DAVID GEARING

SAVIOR

Copyright © 2014 by David Gearing

All rights reserved.

Published 2014 by Akusai Publishing
www.akusaipublishing.com
Cover and layout copyright © 2014 by Akusai Publishing
Cover design by Kevin Johnson
Cover art copyright © Chrobatos/stock.xchng vii

This book is licensed for your personal enjoyment only.
All rights reserved.
This is a work of fiction. All characters and events
portrayed in this book are fictional, and any resemblance
to real people or incidents is purely coincidental. This
book, or parts thereof, may not be reproduced in any
form without permission.

ISBN 13: 978-0615831015
ISBN 10: 061583101X

To my love

Also by David Gearing

Mr. White

Gifted (coming soon)

Echoes (coming soon)

Bloodlines (coming soon)

SAVIOR

ONE

I couldn't bring myself to go to his funeral. That day I refused to be alone, so I walked alone in Wal-Mart in my civilian clothes and traversed across the aisles, shopping for nothing in particular. Children cried for new toys, mothers gasped in excitement over the new spring sales, and I looked at all of the bright and shiny boxes of food and toys and useless crap and tried to push out my memories of Brandon.

My cell phone rang no less than twenty times since eleven o'clock, the time the funeral was supposed to start. I didn't go to the reception either.

The next day, Frank came by my house.

"You didn't show up," he says, takes a seat on my couch and takes a look around my living room. It's relaxed, dark woods with bright red paintings of flowers and houses on the walls. The paintings were Brandon's—my partner's.

"Water? Tea?" I call out from the kitchen.

Frank stands up from the couch as I stick my head out of the kitchen. He walks toward the bookshelf, lined with gritty police dramas and sci-fi novels that Brandon used to love.

"Tea, please," he says. Just as I tuck my head back into the kitchen and open up the refrigerator, I hear the words, "Nice picture."

My hands freeze in place. Splashes of unsweetened tea splats on the floor and I hold my breath. The bitter tea smell tickles the insides of my nose. Which picture is he looking at? My mind's eye runs the gamut of what pictures are sitting out. The eye stops at my mental picture of our vacation photos. Godammit.

I take a quick peek around the corner to see Frank's oversized body near the shelf. In his hands is a golden picture frame, about five by eight. Immediately, I know which one it is. He stares at a picture of me and Brandon holding hands on the beach, walking away from the camera. The picture next to him has me locking lips with Brandon at the same beach. We're leaning against a turquoise metal railing, rusted from the salty ocean air and the sun's rays tickle the sparkly ocean surface.

"Here's your tea," I announce. The shaking cups nearly spill the dark tea on the wooden floors, I'm so nervous. "Do you take sugars?" I ask. I hold the cup out to him, to put the damn picture down.

But it's too late. He's already eyeing the two of us kissing. His eyebrows twitch back and forth, evidence that he's already analyzing, processing, and concluding about the both of us.

"I can explain," I say.

"Two sugars," says Frank. "Please." He takes the cup from my hand, cautious not to spill a single thing. "Thank you," he says. His hand carefully places the picture back on the shelf, right where it was before he discovered my secret, and he paces back to the couch, sits down.

If I could scream right now, I'd shatter glass and cause dogs down the street to lose their minds. The cabinet door is open, but I don't see the spices and sugar sitting in front of me. It's all there, set up for the past three years I've been in this house, but all my mind's eye pictures is Frank asking for my badge and my gun. I see Frank announcing that his detectives suck dick, take it in the ass, and they like it.

I see a helluva lot of thugs and street criminals kicking my ass because they hate faggots.

Frank shouts into the kitchen, "You didn't die in there, did you?"

"N-no," fear trembles my hand to the point that I can't hold anything still, even my other hand. "I just lost the sugar."

Take a deep breath. Get rid of the horrible scenes in my head. Hope for the best, prepare for the worst.

"Oops, there it is!" I shout. Swallowing my worries, everything seems like it's going to go from disappointed to verbally-abused bad.

When I step my right foot into the living room, Frank's large body on my couch draws my gaze. I read his eyebrows, his lips, the creases around his eyes for a sign of emotion. Is he pissed? Indifferent? My career could depend on it.

"Thank you," he says and takes the cup with both hands. He sips the tea, holds it in his mouth for a second and then swallows it like a wine connoisseur. "This is pretty good."

"Ya." That nervous laughter. Pretend you're happy, deny that you're in trouble. "Earl Gray. Good stuff."

"Are you just going to avoid life?" he says. Another sip through his teeth, drawing in a snake-like hiss.

"I'm not avoiding anything," I say.

"You're even avoiding the question," he says. Frank crosses his legs, sits back and clearly feels in control here. "You didn't show up to Brandon's funeral. I respect that it might be too painful.. He was a decent guy. He'll be missed." Another loud hissing sip. "But you can't stay here and pretend that you aren't sad about it."

"I never said I wasn't."

"How about we get you some time off? You've been through a hard time, maybe you need to get your head straight."

"My head is straight." As the word straight leaves my mouth, I wonder when in this conversation the other shoe is going to drop.

"And you need counseling. You know we'll get it for you. Maybe you should talk this out, deal with it."

"I'm fine," I say. I'm still standing near the doorway to the kitchen, putting distance between him and me. It won't matter in this small house, but any distance is better than being so close to him that he can wring my neck.

"No, you're not," he says. Frank blinks, rubs his eyes. "Look, I didn't want to do it this way, but you are going to counseling whether you want it or not. This is not open to discussion." Frank stands up and rests the cup on the end table. "Thank you for the tea." His thick legs take heavy steps to the door, and he turns around to me. "You start tomorrow. Don't come in until you've seen the shrink."

I'll be honest, I don't expect anyone to truly understand. The waiting room at the shrink's office is filled with pale yellow wall paint and a light wood table that makes me think "Dante's tenth level of Hell."

The psych takes me into the room, and we sit down. She offers me something to drink—bottled water—and we sit in silence as she stares at me.

And I can't not stare back at her. Her green eyes blink behind the thin lens bifocals that rest precariously on her nose. "So then I'll start us off," she says. "I understand that you were in quite an accident earlier this week."

This bitch, she thinks she already knows me.

"Ya, quite the incident," I say.

Nearly a year ago from Valentine's Day Brandon and I pulled over a light blue sedan, Ford Fusion, about 1999 model. The car, Brandon said, ran through a light.Brandon made the initial arrest, asking the man to get out of his car, and the woman in the passenger side was crying.

"Sir," said Brandon, "can you get out of the car." He took a step back, hand on his sidearm. I remained as backup by the car, my hands itchy for whatever might about from this.

The man inside the car hesitates and rolls down the windows, a mechanical whir of window and gears. "What the hell are you doing?" he says.

And Brandon loses it. He draws his gun, pulls it out against the man's head and opens it with his right hand.

"Brandon, what are you doing?" I shout at him.

Brandon's green eyes narrow and focus on the man's hands. With nothing more than a turn of his elbow, he pushes the half-naked man against the car and cuffs him.

"You can't do this," he shouts.

"Ma'am, are you okay?" he says. There's a muffled voice inside, and since I'm so far away I don't understand what she says, but Brandon nods and presses the man's cheeks into the roof of the car. "What the fuck were you doing?" he says. "Do you like hurting women?"

The man mutters something in nothing but vowels with his cheeks smashed together, and his jaw pressed down.

"Let the man speak," I say. I step closer to the car, baby steps, to get a better look at the insides. A woman crying, dressed in a not-so-fancy dress with her skirt hanging loose off her knees. Nothing looking distressed or ripped on her. No signs of forced entry. A boy inside, young and maybe sixteen-years-old, and afraid of us. The boy's pants were pulled down entirely, bare-assed and shoving himself into the far corner.

Months later, a grand jury charges the man with attempted rape and exploitation of a minor. In the courtroom, a tall elderly gentleman offers me his hand and then his card and says, "After all of this is over, I'd genuinely like to represent you. Sounds like you'll need it." His suit said I make more money than you'll see in a life time, the shoes were nearly flawlessly new, no dirt and no creases.

Brandon's hands make tight fists, and his jaw tightens up.

"Thank you," I say. I take the card and shove it in my pocket, folding it up. "Yes, he's an asshole, let him go."

The man's card identifies him as Karl Sanderson, Esq. This is the alleged attempted rapist's top lawyer.

Blueblood for sure, but not from Saraday. Not by a long shot. I know all of the influential families here, and he ain't one of them. Where the hell he came from, I don't know. Rumor had it on the prosecution side that he was a family friend.

Some family.

The lawyer sits down next to the alleged rapist. Lays his hands on the shoulder and whispers something into his left ear, paying unusual attention to take a peek at us before he finishes his message.

"You can hit him later," I say. "We'll give him a ticket or something."

After about an hour, we get to listen to the man bitch about how we unfairly singled him out.

"And why do you think you were singled out?" says the lawyer.

The asshole looks at the jurors and then at us. "I don't know. Maybe because we were driving a little fast."

"Would you say that you were driving over the speed limit?" says the lawyer.

Asshole shakes his head no and gets off the stand. Brandon is next.

"Were you aware of what was going on inside the vehicle when you stopped it, officer?"

If you looked closely at Brandon's jaws, you'd

witness them clenching up tight.

"No, I was not aware of anything wrong," he says.

"And you pulled him over because?" says the asshole lawyer. The lawyer faces me, smiles and whispers something that looks like, "Gotcha" in my direction, turns around with his blueblood smile.

Brandon grips the sides of the witness booth with both of his hands, squeezes hard until his knuckles turn bare white. "Because he ran the red light at Maine and Rollercoaster Road."

"And your partner has testified to this?" he says.

Brandon looks at me, then looks down. He knows the answer won't help us now.

Next it was my turn. "What were you and Brandon both doing in the vehicle when only one of you was on duty?"

I gulp and look to Brandon for help. His sad eyes look glossed over and afraid. His lips part just a little, whispering the words, "No. No. No."

"It was just a meeting. We were discussing a previous case." Good job there, Robert. Go with the "I can't talk about current cases" approach.

"I see," says the lawyer. He paces up and down the courtroom. "And do you and Detective Brandon Jones meet up very often?"

And it's times like these I'm happy that he is out

of arm's reach.

"No." Annoyed. Very annoyed.

"And you two have a very long history of working together, don't you?" The lawyer's voice when saying working might as well say homos or faggots.

"Just every once in a while," I say between clenched teeth.

"No more questions, your honor."

The jurors come out of their room, and all stand, then sit at the same time, so synchronized like clockwork.

"Do you have a verdict?" asks the judge.

The juror at the far left stands, with her hands folded neatly in her hands and says, "Not guilty."

"That's bullshit!" shouts Brandon. He stands up in the crowd, points at the jurors and says, "You're kidding me, right?"

The judge's gavel nails the wooden block on his desk, a sharp snap on the desk three times. "I will not have outbursts in my court!" he says.

"Get up," says Brandon. His glance pierces my skin into my brain, commanding me to follow. He stands up, grabbing my shirt and pulls me up. "We're leaving," he says. His forceful steps tap loud into the shocked and solemn courtroom air. "This is complete bullshit," he announces to the court, then lets the heavy wooden door slam behind him.

I, on the other hand, stop at the door, turn and face the court, bow my head because I'll be honest, I don't know what I was supposed to do. So, I shrug and follow Brandon out to the parking lot out front.

"What the hell was that?" he says. His shoulders rise up, tense. "Are you trying to destroy our careers?"

The thought never crossed my mind. I'm speechless.

"You could have gotten us kicked off the force."

"We didn't get the guy," I say. "I had to do something."

"Are you fucking stupid?" Brandon's face is close to mine. His nose, a slight Roman-hooked nose that adds a classic handsomeness to his profile, it's close to mine and it's everything I could do to keep from kissing him right then and there. "We can't be," he stops, looks around. Brandon whispers, "Together."

"Apparently we're not," I say.

"And just how did that make you feel?" says the psychologist.

"Paranoid as hell," I say. "How would you feel if you had to deny the person you loved in public?"

"And was that stressful?" she says.

No, not stressful at all. "What do you think?" I say. "I'm here, aren't I?"

"You're here for another matter altogether, Robert." She tips her glasses back and takes a drink from a glass on the desk next to her. If I were her, that clear liquid would be vodka. My nose tells me it's some raspberry flavored health water.

That next week we fought over stupid stuff. He tried to avoid me, but somehow ran into me everywhere he went. The more he saw me, the more he apparently couldn't resist me. I couldn't tell if I was following him, or he was following me. He was probably in the same confusion.

A week after not seeing each other as a couple—but still running into each other everywhere—we decided we would go get some food together. His feelings didn't change, and mine were stronger. I made the moves, put my hand on his hand when we went to the car in the parking lot. That's all it took and he finished the move with a kiss on the mouth.

After that, we moved in together, Brandon and me. He brought some of his stuff over to my place, and we settled the rest of his living room furniture into an air-conditioned storage unit.

Our shifts were only a few hours apart, so we left the house together, got some breakfast. Brandon left before I did, and he got home a little bit before I did. He usually had dinner on the table when I got home. He was remarkable that way.

"And everything was great?" says the psychiatrist.

"Everything was wonderful while it lasted."

"What prompted you to move in together?" she says, jots down a few notes.

"We figured we might as well. He stayed over five out of seven nights a week. We had fun, we cared about each other, and we had similar shifts. It just worked out that way."

"A relationship of convenience?" asks the psychiatrist.

"Convenient for who?" I say. "Being a cop is hard. It's nice to have someone who understands that."

A month after Brandon moved in, he decides that we needed to take a quick trip to the grocery store. "It's a surprise," he says and smiles at me while we're on the side roads going in some such direction. The moon hangs overhead in a bright half circle, waxing, and illuminating the clouds that creep past it. The rolled down windows reveal the mating cries of frogs and birds of the night all around us.

"No, seriously," I say. "Where are we going?"

"We'll see," he says.

The car pulls off to a side road that leads to a subdivision surrounded by sparse pockets of trees and large green fields that are probably parts of a golfing green in the daylight. I keep my quiet and pretend that I know what's going on. The street lights blink yellow and orange onto the road, illuminating the inside of the car in bright circles that come and go into the night behind us.

"What is this?" I say.

"Remember that case?" he says. Brandon's face turns to serious, each muscle becomes stiff as stone. He glares hard into my eyes.

I nod.

"We're going to check on something," he says. "An old hunch."

Hunches were Brandon's way of saying that he got a lead from somewhere and wanted to take all the credit for himself. His hunches went from finding burgled items to discovering when surprise birthday parties were to be thrown in his honor. His idea of hunches was really a game of mental cat-and-mouse. "You can't keep anything from me."

"Another hunch?" I say. "Who tipped you off?"

Brandon grabs my leg and squeezes.

Brandon kills the headlights and drives down the street at a four miles per hour.

"Who are we stalking?" I say.

Brandon doesn't answer, but keeps his eyes to a house to the far corner. The house is blue. Big wooden door. We park about one hundred feet down the street and get out of the car.

"Is this some kind of surprise party?" I ask.

Brandon pulls his gun from the back of his jeans and shakes his head "no".

"Goddammit, Brandon, what is this?"

"Just follow me," he says. Brandon storms the door with a true purpose, his right hand on the grip of his gun.

"We don't really need a gun," I say, but really ask.

Brandon doesn't knock, and the door creaks open when Brandon pushes it open. "Are you ready?"

It's habit that makes me grab for my nonexistent gun. Not being on duty, I left my firearm at home. "Sure, why not?"

Brandon points his gun to the floor and walks slowly into the house. He says nothing, and as I open my mouth to say, "Excuse me," he stops me with a cold stare, eyes narrowed. I bite my tongue so hard I should have been tasting the iron in my blood.

He takes steps—slow steps—down the dark wooden hallway, pointing his gun at each of the doors. The baby blue plush carpeting silences our sneaking and clashes with the walls. "Are we giving them decorating advice?" I ask. He doesn't take the joke.

"Clear," he says.

"Brandon," I whisper, but apparently not loud enough for him to hear. "Where the hell are we?"

"Right here," Brandon says. He rests his ear to the door, squints his eyes and listens. His face turns sour, and his mandible joints pop out at the cheeks as he gnashes his teeth together.

"The fuck, Brandon?" His size eleven-foot kicks in the door and Brandon raises his gun up and toward two men.

"What the hell are you doing?" says Asshole. He reaches for his pants just hanging off his ankles.

The boy is reaching for the pillows on the bed, hiding his head deep into the centers, lost in the feathery marshmallow at the head of his bed. Something else strikes me as I watch Brandon take Asshole off the boy and slam him up against the wall. The room is all blue, baby blue with pictures of sports cars and baseball players on the wall. Framed pictures of the boy wearing a striped baseball uniform, smiling triumphantly into the camera. In his hand, the same trophy that sits on a shelf across the room.

"This is your own son?" I say.

"Step son," says the boy. He rolls over and pulls down his shirt. His legs, however, lie spread eagle across the bed, testicles and dick laying flat against his leg. "And I'm 18, assholes. Leave him alone."

The boy has a slight lisp the way he says assholes and I cringe. It's people like this that give us a bad name.

"You have the right to remain silent," says Brandon. He presses Asshole harder into the wall. Asshole's ass is bare against the front of Brandon's pants, but Brandon leans in and pushes his mouth to Asshole's left ear and whispers something.

"No, please," Asshole cries. "Please, don't."

"What are we doing here, Brandon?" I ask. My hands stay up to reveal that I don't have a weapon. Hands up into the air, chest-level, I back up to the doorway. "We should probably go."

"Fuck that," Brandon says. "You know what he did to us."

"You're the fucking cops?" says Asshole. "You?" Asshole laughs, and it looks like his shoulders relax against the wall as his hands fall flat and limp.

"Good," says Brandon. "You remember."

"Listen, man," says Asshole. "We're good. We're even. Just let me go. Cool?"

"Not cool," says Brandon, followed by a click.

"What the hell are you doing, Brandon," I say. "We need to go." I swallow spit, and an oncoming panic attack when I realize that the boy is sliding off the bed gradually toward me. "Stay there," I say.

The boy runs at me, charging as fast as his socked feet can gain traction on the hardwood floors. When a naked young man is running at you, your first reaction is to move, in case you were wondering. Instead of crashing right into me, he hits the wall in the hallway behind me and continues running down the hallway.

"Brandon, this is getting out of hand," I say.

"Listen to your boyfriend," says Asshole. His grunts something like a laugh and says, "You guys should really leave." Brandon's right elbow pushes into the man's back shoulder, presses hard. "I'll fucking own you. I'll fucking own your whole department," says Asshole.

Brandon beats the man in syllables with the end of the gun's handle. "Shut. The. Fuck. Up." The last swing of the gun causes the man to collapse at Brandon's feet.

He takes a step back, broadening his stance and

says, "Get up."

"Brandon, don't you think this is a bit drastic?" I say. I take a few steps forward, but not too close. Can't risk setting off either Brandon or Asshole. "We can charge him with this, I'm sure."

"I said I'm eighteen," says the boy from behind me. Before I can turn around, I hear a creaking of the floorboards from the hallway and a thud.

A piercing fire grazes across my right shoulder. My hand grabs the area and pulls back with a slick red warmth. A step to the side, and my training makes me reach for my nonexistent firearm yet again.

The floorboards creak again as the boy comes into the room, points his gun straight at Brandon. From here I can witness his wrists shaking from the nerves, maybe from firing the first shot, I don't know. What I can tell is, the boy isn't skilled enough to aim and shoot at anything with extreme accuracy.

"Brandon, watch out!" I shout at my partner.

Brandon's back turns to Asshole and then slams into him with one more BAM! Another bullet from the gun enters Brandon's left side and exits through Asshole's shoulder.

Brandon drops to his knees...

"...and I'm powerless. I can't move, I can't see, I can't hear anything, and that's what I remembered from that evening," I say.

The psychologist clicks her pen against the notepad on her lap and she scribbles something down onto the page. "And how does your shoulder feel now?"

Her frown suggests real interest, not the fake stuff you hear at the supermarket when you ask someone to grab the cereal from the top shelf because your deltoids are still healing. "It only hurts when I laugh," I joke. She doesn't get it, or at least doesn't laugh.

"And the boy?" says the psychologist. "What happened to him?"

TWO

The shrink hands me a white business card that reads DR. PHYLLIS ROSS, M.D. I flick the edges of the card with my index finger twice, three times, before I tuck it into my pocket.

"Please, Robert," Dr. Ross says to me, "call if you need to talk about anything."

I nod back to her and thank her. "I'll be fine." When I get back home, I'll most likely forget that I had that card in my pocket. It'll end up as a tangled ball of wet pulp in the washer, then dried to a crispy ball of dust in the dryer. Because I can't pay attention to almost anything. I have to force myself to have a regular life. Because all I can think about his him.

A glass door and a sterile white foyer exits outside to a bright, burning sun. My dry skin on my back itches from a combination of heat and the polyester of my white undershirt. My car—not the squad car—waits for me patiently right where I left it. If I drove the squad car, I could park it nearly anywhere. Nice thing about being a cop: traffic laws don't apply to us. But this time, I don't need to stand out. I'm trying to blend in and pretend that I'm not a cop. Just regular civilian Robert Lambert. No badge. No gun. No worries.

As if.

I'm hungry, so I stop at the local burrito shop, a taqueria that sells breakfast burritos all day. The lady behind the counter, a young light-skinned Hispanic with her hair pulled up into a ponytail that bounces, almost dances as she tries to pronounce everything in English. "One burrito, meester?"

I hand over a crumpled five dollar bill and wait. A young couple, in love and groping each other around their waists, pulls the door open and stumbles in. They order together in that sickening way, never letting go of the other's hips. Like it's a game to them. See who can last the longest without letting go. I swallow my pride and my instinct to yell at them and look the other direction. And in this mirror is a man reflected back at me. He blinks when I blink, and he looks so suddenly old. Dark circles around his eyes reveal nights of barely getting any sleep. The way his skin looks blotchy tells me that he's been sweating and straining and utterly out of his routine. Even his shirt is untucked, and his shoulders are hunched over.

This is what I look like. My sad eyes dilate further as I try to focus on my brown-black hair that was combed earlier this morning. I swear, though you'd never know if you looked at it now.

"Meesta sir?" says the lady with a brown bag of breakfast burrito. She holds it up and offers it to me though I'm barely paying any attention at all to her. I can only think, as a detective I'm trained to learn about people, to know who they are and why they behave how they do. I've seen that face—my face—so many times in the mornings and afternoons over these past thirty years. Yet, as I stand here in this fluorescent-lit restaurant, I barely recognize those eyes and that hair and that blotchy skin.

Brandon would barely recognize me either.

I thank the lady for the burrito and peer inside the bag. She was kind enough to include the green salsa in the tiny clear plastic tubs. As I sit in the car and stare back into the restaurant through the front window, the smells of spice and sweet bacon drifts up my nose and my stomach tries to grumble but it can't. It doesn't want to because eating something right now means that I have to feel something. Feeling something doesn't seem like a good idea. I want to be numb. I need to be empty. I need to get away and stop thinking. But I know how successful I'll be at that.

I unwrap the burrito with my left hand and try to keep the juice and sauce from dripping with my right. The burrito tastes empty and dry, all potato and not enough egg. Just enough bacon to make me want more bacon. My bites get bigger and bigger as I realize that I'm far hungrier than I thought. Turns out the best part of this entire burrito is that it sucks up the spicy verde sauce without any problems. No dripping means no explanations about stains when I go in and talk to the captain in a half hour.

Things that scare the hell out of a grown ass man.

This is the conversation that will determine whether I get to come back to my regular job or to a desk job. This is the conversation that already makes the butterflies in my stomach regurgitate their food. I'm that nervous.

When the chips fall during this meeting, I just hope everything falls in my favor.

There are pros and cons to sitting at a desk job, but most of the pros can be outdone with the abject humiliation that comes with the assignment. Being a desk jockey isn't exactly glorious. It's not what I served in the force for years and tested year after year to get to. I did not carry a gun and ride the beat so I could just sit still and stamp papers all day. It's not what I'm about, and it's not what I wanted out of my life.

Still, there's safety to consider. There's PTSD, according to the psychiatrist. There's thoughts of revenge and memories and their fears that I'm just going to pull a gun in public and shoot everyone I see. It's the irrational that keeps them worried.

Secretly, I guess I worry about them too.

After all, one pull of the trigger and I can end my own problems. I can make them all go away and be with Brandon again. It's just a gun click away.

But that's not genuinely what anyone wants. It's not what Brandon would want. What Mom wants, or what Dad wants.

But really, it's what I want that matters, dammit. And as of now, I have no idea what that is. Nothing is realistic. Nothing seems appealing. I'm not even sure I want this burrito.

But I finish it anyway.

Just after I'm done celebrating my last bite with a deep belly, green chili burp, the Latino couple comes out of the restaurant still smiling. They are holding hands and in love. I want to yell, "Get a room." Flash my badge and take them in for lewd public acts. Disturbing the peace. Something official sounding that they won't contest.

Instead, I turn the ignition and back out of the parking lot. As I pull out onto the street, the clouds up above travel in toward the hills and get dark real fast. The way Saraday weather is, this summer's shower will be a doozy. We haven't had a heavy rain in a few days. In a humid subtropical environment, that's nearly unheard of.

But in Saraday, nothing should seriously surprise you.

Last week we got a call about a boy who was speaking in tongues and harassing his neighbor's cat. The day before that, we had to arrest two boys for blowing up an outhouse.

Yes, I said outhouse.

Then just the other day a young woman went missing amidst a fire in a bar. No corpse. No bones. No signs of foul play. Just missing.

Welcome to Saraday.

I travel up I-95 for two exits and get off next to the police station. We've been stationed there since the old police building was destroyed in the Great Fire. This town, it's got a crazy history that makes me wonder if our families didn't build it on top of some ancient Indian burial ground or something.

The parking lot is nearly empty with civilian cars. Our white and freshly washed squad cars lined up like obedient little soldiers are ready for duty. So military and so clean.

My boss is waiting for me at my desk. His feet are up on my calendar, which is blank. The bottoms of his shoes are clean and still a hard plastic, no sign of wear. No rocks stuck in the grooves.

"What's up, boss?" I say. I grin, let him know I'm having a fabulous day despite what my eyes tell him.

Not that he doesn't look much better. "Don't bullshit me," he says. If Andy Griffith and a walrus had a child and shoved him in police blues, you'd get our lovable captain. His thick walrus-like mustache is something of a legend around the office. It moves when he talks and when he finds some food in it after lunch, Capt. Frank affectionately refers to it as his "Flavor Saver."

Frank inherited a giant mess when he took over as Captain from Sumter, South Carolina. A small town boy from a suburb of Charleston, Frank was what you could call Old School. He went to church twice a week on Sundays and Wednesdays, only goes to "membership only' bars, and refuses to give up hope when things go horribly wrong. He'll also stay in this job until some old woman can talk him into retiring.

And we're all waiting for that day to come real soon. The women in the department—all three of them—set him up on a date about a dozen times. None of them worked out, as you can tell.

Still, that doesn't seem to keep Captain Frank in a poor disposition.

"Get your ass in here and quit dawdlin'!"

His office consists of little except dark wood walls and black frames various certificates, awards, and thank you letters from all of the schools in the county. I take a seat and shuffle my feet back and forth, first crossing them one way, then another.

"So?" he says.

A massive migration of butterflies takes flight in my stomach. "So, uh," I say. My mind goes blank, and I see that Frank isn't in a humoring kind of mood today. His moustache drapes over his upper lip and most of his lower lip, giving a pissed off kind of frown. "She says I'm okay," I say. "Not perfect, but okay."

"Is that so?" the captain says. He rests his ass on the oxblood leather rolling desk chair and peers at me over the rims of his glasses. "Why do I feel like I don't believe you?" he says.

"You didn't get the report?" I ask. "I swear I saw

her fax it over."

Frank looks at his desk, shuffles a few papers around and shakes his head. "Nope, not here."

"Can you call?" I ask. I think about all of the resources I can exhaust here. I need to be back out there. I can't go back into a desk job. A leave of absence would be me lying on the bed, staring at all of his shit.

"I'm not calling because I don't see that I have to," Frank says. His feet touch the ground once more and he sits forward, the light reflecting off his skull. His brow throws shade over the rest of his face, all ghost story like, and he says to me, "You're taking a few days off, I think. Serve you good."

"But, sir," I say. My hands hit the desk. Fire dwells in my belly, threatens to come charging out of my throat as I yell back, "I am not going on vacation."

"Oh so now you get some bass in your voice," says Frank with a smile. "It's a shame you didn't do that in court. Your partner would still be alive."

"You sonuva—"

"You won't finish that sentence if you know what's good for you, Lambert. Not. Another. Single. Syllable." Frank's index finger hovers a hair's breath away from my nose. "You're a good man, and decent cop," he says, pulling his finger back and resting against the desk. "That's the only reason why I'm letting you go with a warning here."

"I don't know what to say," I tell him. I can't look up at him, can't show my rage and shame and everything in between.

"It's probably best you don't say anything, Lambert," he says. "We'll see you in about a week. We clear, Lambert?" he says. Frank sits down in his chair and rests back, comfortable. Makes me picture him immediately as an 80's era mob-boss.

"Crystal. Sir." I take a few steps back and turn around. As my hand grips the door, my gut tells me to speak up, tell him I'm sorry. Instead, I grip the round metal knob tightly and turn to open the door.

THREE

Despite my best wishes, the rest of the office turns and looks at me leaving Frank's office. There's something about having two dozen people freeze-tag still while you're trying to be as inconspicuous as possible. It's intimidating, to say the least.

"How's it going?" says Hernandez. Officer Lana Hernandez, our heart and soul and the person who can feel someone's pain from miles away, her eyes analyze my mood, searching from left to right. Her eyes read mine, the creases in and around my eye sockets. They search my lips and the ends of them to see just how sad I just might be. "You okay?" she asks.

I nod and mumble something that sounds like "Thank you" but even I'm not sure. My mind is not what you'd call clear.

I go to my desk and pull out the chair but don't sit. Everything has been spotless for weeks, no papers on my desk, everything filed away. No dust, no pencils, no coffee stains on the calendar. Perfection.

This isn't my doing, believe me.

Instead, this is the doing of the officers around the department. Saraday being a small town, we look after our own whenever something horrible happens. We're a tight-knit community. It's comforting in most cases, but not mine.

Mine is an exception, an exhausting exception that has caused me too much grief in the past and the here-and-now of it all.

Hernandez rests her ass against my desk, and with her most sincere apologetic face she can muster, she says, "Did Frank put you on desk duty?"

I shake my head "no." "Leave of absence," I say.

"Well that might be good, huh? Being out of here for a while? It can't be easy losing your partner."

She doesn't know the half of it.

"Listen," I say. "I just need to get a few things and get out of here." I take an unframed photograph out from my left desk drawer, the one I use to store all of the bullshit clips and pins. The three by five picture fits squarely into the palm of my hand as I cup it to keep it out of Hernandez's eyes. I close the drawer. "I'll see you around sometime."

Hernandez reaches her tiny arms around my broad shoulders and tries her best to make her hands touch. Fingertip to fingertip, she squeezes my chest and lets out a playful moan. "Just take care of yourself, okay, buddy?"

"Sure thing," I say and push her back.

I take care to not stand out and look at anyone else as I leave the building. The sun has been baking the insides of my car for nearly a half hour by now, and the ninety degree heat with eighty-five percent humidity is not fun for anyone. It's the warm, moist, just-got-out-of-the-shower feeling you love at first, but get to dry off. In South Carolina, it's a mainstay of the summers.

I thank God once again that I had the foresight to buy a car with fabric seats as I sit down and start the ignition once again. When the ignition starts, I begin this mental conversation with myself.

"Where am I supposed to go?"

"Home is too depressing."

"Can't stay at work. Frank doesn't want you there."

"I could see a movie, I guess."

"But that would require money you don't want to

spend."

The voices argue it out as I pull into the street and decide I'll take backroads to keep from forcing a decision from either of the voices.

The first giant bug-like splats on my window fall from the sky. Then another. And another, until the clouds up above empty their contents on us poor drivers. The clouds hang dark in the sky. Thick black puffs of water vapor that grow so large they have begun to shield out the sun.

My brain's autopilot takes firm control over the driving of the car while the inner voices work out the pros and cons of going to see a movie. Just as soon as Voice One is about to speak his mind about what movies are out, I come across the bridge, and the rain comes down in torrential downpours. A curtain of rain falls from the heavens, nailing every square inch of the car in metallic harmony. As much as I love the sound and smell of rain, I wish the Carolina skies would make it easier for us to see the streets.

My visibility is probably somewhere in the range of ten feet in front of the car. It's enough to go somewhere, but not good enough to get there safely.

I consider pulling over before I get to the bridge that crosses the Low Country River just outside of town. It's the longest and most scenic way back to my house for a change of clothes before I run back outside and see whatever movie Voice One and Voice Two agree on.

I tap the brakes as I approach the bridge and roll into a complete stop. In our exceptionally rainy season, this bridge washes out completely, and it's impossible to drive further into this part of town. The branches bend from the torrent up above and the large splatters on the street make me rethink my whole plan here.

Maybe it's best to just pull over.

When I put the transmission back into drive, a moving shadow catches my eye and flick on the high beams of my car, drive in reverse to turn the beams around to the edges of the bridge. Amidst the gray shadow of rain, a figure moves back and forth, dark and fairly bulky. A dog? A bear?

I pull the car forward to get a better look. The headlights reveal a human figure standing on the edge of the bridge, facing outward and staring off into the distance.

This really can't be happening. Not now.

I roll down the window and shove my head out into the rain. As I shout into the storm that this person needs to get inside the car right now, a crack of thunder announces that a bolt of lightning simultaneously struck nearby. "Hey!" I shout again. "You really don't want to be out here."

The rain lightens up as I open the door. I let one foot out, nice and slow, thinking that any jumpy moves might startle the fellow, and we'd be fishing him out of the river below.

"Hey there!" I say. I hold my hands up to caution this person that I'm not a threat. "Do you need a ride?" I ask. "Do you think you can come down from there, and we can talk?" I say. At the end of every sentence, my black dress shoes squeak on the wet street. I know this person hears me. I stop and survey the situation. This person's right tennis shoe hangs off the ledge. The person is wearing loose-fitting blue jeans—now soaked black—which means this person is a he. The black jacket hoodie that hangs off this young man's shoulders drapes past his butt, his hands are not long enough to come out of the sleeves. He stands maybe five-feet-five. Definitely a teenager. "C'mon, young man, why don't we talk about this?"

What this is, I don't know. I don't want to lose another person. Not on my day off.

And though the rain has lightened up, I can barely see the subtle movement of the boy's hood turning at me. The fleshy point of his nose turns to his left, his nostril flares as he shows me a big, goofy grin.

"C'mon, sir," I say. I can't use the word boy because

sometimes that gets taken the wrong way, especially by suicidal and temperamental young teenagers. The phrase young man could have also been a viable option. "You can step off, and we can fix whatever it is that's wrong." I take a step toward the boy, inch by inch so that he doesn't see me make these steps. The last thing I need is for him to think I'm going to grab him.

I mean, it's what I'm going to do, but he doesn't need to know that.

The boy's leg drifts over the ledge again, moving back and forth. Teasing me. He's letting me know that he's serious, but if he was really that serious, he would have jumped by now.

After inching my way up to him, I've made a good six or seven feet gap between him and me. If I needed to get him, to rescue him, I could do so with a little bit of effort. Not impossible, but not easy.

"Just give me your hand," I say.

The boy, he puts both of his feet back on the ledge.

"That's it, just come on down nice and easy." I take my hand and extend it out to grab him, to support his weight for when he decides to come on down and join the rest of the living.

Then, my worst nightmare prepares to jumpstart my heart.

The boy's knees bend, but his feet are held close

together. His arms, they swing backward, and he bends over slightly at the waist.

This little fucker's going to jump.

"You don't have to do that," I say. "Come on down. I promise we can get you help." I take a few steps toward him again in larger steps. Right at this moment, I don't care if he manages to hear me or see me. I don't care if I scare him. He needs to be rescued.

He wants to be rescued.

I need to rescue him.

When the boy's jacket pushes out from behind him as he bends over, I grab its tail and pull as hard as I can. The boy's hold on the ledge is impressive, and it takes a lot of shoulder strength to tug him down and back onto the bridge next to me.

I tug, twisting my torso and gritting my teeth together, like that's going to help me.

The boy's footing collapses backward along with the rest of his body and he lands in my chest, pushing me backward.

This is when his weight becomes too much for my thirty-year-old body, and I feel gravity pull me backwards and downwards. My arms wrap fully around the boy. If I can keep my body underneath his, I can keep him from being injured.

Must keep him in grasp.

Tight hold.

Can't flee.

Get him safe.

Brace for impact.

When I curl my body together, I realize that I'm really keeping him cuddled in my grip. The boy, his body relaxes as he rests in mine. I'm his human safety net.

"Are you okay?" I say after taking a second to catch my breath. "Are you hurt?"

The boy says nothing, but his face has a twisted smile. His eyes closed tight, locks of dirty blond hair escapes his hood. Everything about this boy says that he must have been on the streets for quite some time.

I pull myself out from under him and check his pulse and his chest. He's breathing. Blood is pumping at what feels like normal BPM.

Shaking him causes his hood to slide down the back of his head to reveal long hair that hasn't been cut in a couple of weeks, at least.

"Hey kid." Shake his shoulders and check for a response. "You okay?" Shake a little more. "Kid?"

The boy raises his eyebrows, which pulls his eyelids open.

"Are you okay?" I ask again, this time slower in case he doesn't speak English. Or he's deaf. Or something.

"Hello?"

The boy smacks my hand away with his and pulls himself up. His hair whips back and forth as he peers left, the right, then up at the sky. I follow his gaze and look up, too. Maybe this kid's mothership is about to land.

"Do you got a name?"

The boy shakes his head and looks over his shoulder at me directly into my eyes. He waves his hands over his eyes—ice blue eyes—to push his bangs back up to his forehead.

"Don't you?" says the boy. His voice cracks as he says "you" and I think I might have to reevaluate my age approximation. He pushes his weight up off the ground, and he stands on his tennis-shoed feet and stares back at me. His stares, there's something I don't like about them. I get the creepy feeling that he's not looking at me, he's looking through me.

My initial reaction is to look behind me, see maybe what he's staring at.

"Nice try," I tell him with a smile. "But I can't let you run off just yet." Standing up and listening to the ass muscles creak, I ask him, "Your name, do you mind telling me what it is?"

This boy smiles at me. My bones feel cold when he does this. He's playing with me and doesn't seem the least bit bothered by my saving him.

"Joey," he says. The boy pulls his hood back up over his head, and it throws a shadow over his forehead and top bridge of his nose. "What's yours, officer?"

"I'm Detective Lambert," I say. I extend my hand. "You can call me Robert."

"Sure thing, Robbie," he says. His hands disappear into his large jacket pockets, and he moves quick and graceful to the car and opens the passenger side door. "I'm hungry," he says. "How about you?"

FOUR

It's not that I want to go home, I just don't want to babysit. I've come to terms with never having kids of my own. It's just not a reality in my life at this point. I have no one to help raise the kids. My career is dangerous and requires long hours and frequently long shifts.

I wander about the streets disciplining the public. The last thing I want to do is come home and discipline my own kids. Or kid. Or…whatever.

Joey waits for me to open the passenger side front door and he says, "Thank you." My opinion of him changes when he simply leaves me behind and walks into the building to get a table.

By the time I walk into the door of Little Teapot Café, Joey isn't waiting for me. The wooden sign attached to the register in front commands in large gold letters that we PLEASE WAIT TO BE SEATED.

The register has been abandoned. Young and old ladies alike in white aprons bother each of the tables in their sections. More coffee? More orange juice?

"Uh, excuse me," I say and try to flag down one of the younger waitresses. "Can you tell me if you've seen a little boy?" I put my hands up to about my chest. "About yay tall?"

The waitress looks at me and says, "Oh, I'll be just a minute, you sit tight."

She didn't call me officer. She didn't notice a badge or a gun. She didn't recognize that I sit here every lunch hour four days a week.

I check my chest, my hips, and short sleeves for signs of cop uniform. Did I accidentally pin on a badge or nametag? No stripes. No plastic pins. No holster and no gun means I'm in civilian garb. Means I shouldn't be able to be identified as a cop.

But how did he know?

The waitress pulls out a laminated menu, tucks it under her arm and says to me, "Just you today?"

"Uh, no, I," and I stop talking. He's not here. But

I did come in with a little boy. "Did you seat a little teenage boy, blond hair? Black jacket?"

The waitress squints and looks up, her eyes look to the upper left corner of her eye sockets. She's left-brained. Analytical, linear thinker. Probably decent at math, gets numbers. "No, I didn't seat anyone," she says, and her head whips around to survey the dining room. "But that doesn't mean someone didn't do it earlier."

"He would have just walked in maybe a second ago."

The waitress shrugs, look at me. "Dunno."

I identify a pale hand waving from a black jacket in my peripheral vision. The waitress sees him, too.

"I think I spotted him," I tell her and ignore the offer for a menu.

"I'll let Jenny know you're on 27," she says and holds out the menu anyway despite me just walking away from her.

"What was that?" I ask Joey. His nose is buried deep in his menu, held high enough to block my line of sight to his eyes and nose.

"I was waving to tell you where I was," he says. "Are they still selling breakfast?"

I take the menu from his hands. "Look at me." The room feels nearly five degrees colder when his ice blue eyes grab ahold of mine. "This isn't funny."

"I never said I was trying to be." He holds out his hand and waves his fingers toward him. "Can I have that back?"

The young waitress—Carolyn, by the name on her nametag—comes into the room to check on us. "You forgot this," she says and drops the menu onto the table. The air underneath it cushions the impact onto the table and delivers it over to Joey's side of the table. He picks it up, gives me a great bit "Gotcha!" type of smile and buries is nose back into the menu. "Did you guys need anything to drink?" says Carolyn.

"Water and a coffee. Black," I say. I take the seat that lies directly between Joey and the only door out of here.

"Coffee, three sugars," says Joey. "And can I just get a bowl of those little cream thingies?"

"Sure thing, sugar," says Carolyn. She jots something down on her green pad. "Are you ready to order food?"

"I need a minute," I say, but Joey interrupts me.

"Are you still serving breakfast?"

This pain in the ass is trying his hardest to be cute to the waitress, who is probably five years older than him. I guess you can't blame a boy for trying.

"We serve breakfast all day," she says.

"Could you come back in a few minutes?" I ask.

Carolyn puts her pad in the front pocket of her apron and smiles as she walks away.

"Stop being like this."

"Like what?" he asks.

I grab the top of the menu closest to me and push it down onto the table. Nothing but ketchup and mustard bottles and salt and pepper shakers stand between me and him. I know he sees me. "Being so rude to me," I say through my teeth. "I'm only trying to help."

Joey's eyes look up, thinking. "I don't remember saying anything about needing help."

"So you weren't just trying to kill yourself back there?"

"That bridge hangs over a river," he says. "Do you really think I was going to die?" He shrugs, playing with me. "Maybe I just wanted to swim."

This. This here is why I don't have kids.

"Don't be cute," I say.

"You'd like that, wouldn't you." He winks at me. My face stays still, calm. I can't show a reaction, can't let him get to me.

"I meant to her," I say. The waitress comes in with two sand-colored mugs in her left hand, lets them down easy on the tabletop. In her other hand, she pours a thick stream of black coffee into both mugs and taps the ceramic container with white, yellow, and pink sugar packets on the table.

"That's for you," she says, looking at Joey. "I'll be back with the creamer."

"Thank you," says Joey. He flashes his blue eyes at her, cartoon-vixen style. This is just a game to him.

"I said cut that out." The bitter coffee once it touches my lips makes me wish I ordered extra creamer and more sugar packets. For now, I grab a few packets and tap them against the back of my right thumb. "So tell me about yourself," I say. This boy's eyes, they blink a few times, and I'm instantly drawn into them as he begins to speak in short sentences, avoiding everything I try to get out of him.

"I'm Joey," he begins. He stirs his coffee and looks up at the pictures of yellow and blue flowers hanging on the walls. "I'm about sixteen years old."

"About sixteen?" I ask. Make mental notes about this kid in secret. If I can keep him from thinking that I'm building a dossier on him, then maybe I can get him to open up and talk more.

"About," he says, thinking for a second and then nodding in agreement. "I'd say that's about right."

"Where are you from?" I ask. "Where's your family?"

"I'm from here," says Joey. He takes another long

slurp of coffee. "I've lived here all my life. My family, though." He stirs his coffee, takes another white sugar packet and dumps the contents, and stirs. "I don't know where they are."

"How do you not know?" I ask. "Did you run away?"

"No," he says. "They moved away."

"What? While you were gone?"

"Ya, like that," he says.

Carolyn's face looks worn down, droopy. She offers a weary smile to welcome us. "So have you boys thought about ordering?" She readies her pen and taps it on the pad.

"I'll just have two eggs. Scrambled. Two slices of bacon and rye toast."

Carolyn nods at me and then looks to Joey, "And for you, sir?"

"How about a stack of pancakes. Eggs. Over-easy. Hash browns. And toast," he says, then nudges the cup toward the edge of the table. "And more coffee."

"No problem," says Carolyn. "Is white bread okay?" she asks.

Joey says, "Yes, and thank you," and watches as the waitress prances away from us.

"So you can say thank you," I mutter.

"Yes, I can say thank you," he says. "But you didn't

earn it, officer."

"Can we cut the crap?" I ask. I lean further over the table and whisper in a low voice. "Just how did you know that I'm a cop?" I ask.

"I don't know what you mean," he says. He looks at the coffee cup, then at me. "How do you mean, officer?"

"Detective."

Joey raises an eyebrow. "What?"

"I'm a detective," I say. "But you called me officer just now, and then back there at the bridge." Carolyn and gives us both a refill and then smiles as she wanders away to help another table somewhere. "How did you know?"

"I've seen you around," he says. Joey shrugs and grabs another three or four—I've lost count—sugar packets of all colors and rips them open. The white contents cascade into the black coffee and swirl down, slow and heavy.

"I don't believe you," I say. "How did you know?"

"That's not really important right now," he says. "Sugar?

"Put those down," I demand. "And stop playing around." I sit back in the chair, try to demand that I have the control in this conversation. "When we're done eating, we're taking you back to your parents."

Joey smiles at me and says, "Good luck."

"What's that supposed to mean?" I ask.

"Nothing."

For the next fifteen minutes, I let him eat in peace. No questions, no comments, no worries. This nut is a tough one to crack, so I try what I can to make him relax and get him to open up. Right now, maybe he just needs to be left alone.

But that doesn't stop my brain from flurrying into a dozen different scenarios. What I see in my mind's profile of this kid is a boy who didn't like his fatherly figure. A boy who rebelled whenever he could. The rebel without a clue. Then, when things got too rough, his parents kicked him out, and he lived on the streets.

Maybe he just saw me around town, saw me in a squad car. Saw me flashing the lights on the street and recognized who I was. Maybe.

He doesn't eat voraciously, so I figure he's had food from time to time. The way he holds the fork, gripping the whole fork with his whole fist, the pronged end sticking out past his index finger and thumb, makes me think he's shoveling the food into his mouth. Maybe he wasn't taught a proper way to hold the fork. He's not from money.

Joey drops his fork on the plate to announce that he's done eating and wipes his mouth with the napkin and drops it on the plate. "Can I get dessert?"

"No, you cannot. First you need to tell me where I can drop you off."

"I can't do that. They don't live there anymore," he says. "We went over this."

"We didn't go over anything. You've been tight-lipped on this whole thing." I pat my mouth dry with the napkin and look at him, but his eyes keep trying to steal my attention. So, looking over his head, I say, "We need to sort this whole thing out. You can either tell me where you live, or I can take you down to county courts, and we can figure out what to do with you then."

"You drive a hard bargain, Robbie."

"Don't call me that. That's Detective Robert to you."

"Are you afraid to die?" he says.

"Is that supposed to be a threat?" I ask him.

"It's a perfectly legit question, officer—"

"Detective," I interrupt.

He pauses, corrects himself. "Detective." He takes a breath and continues, "I mean, you're in a pretty dangerous profession there."

"Let's change the topic."

"So why did you become a cop?" Joey continues. His eyes pierce into me, and I think to myself that I must have seen those eyes before.

I must have blocked it all out already.

"To serve and protect," I tell him. I need to regain control of this conversation.

"To serve who? Protect who? A gun can only truly protect yourself," says Joey. He slurps the rest of the coffee out of the mug and slides it over to his left. He's clearly done with the coffee but just beginning on me.

"Protect whom," I correct. "To serve and protect whom. What do they teach you in school?"

"You're dodging my question, Robbie."

"I'm not the center of attention here. You are." I point my pen in his face and pull the pocket-sized spiral-bound notebook out of my shirt and turn to a clean page.

"So you're scared of death?" says Joey. There's this serene calm in Joey's voice as he says this, something that chills me. I shiver and tell myself that the air conditioning must have just come on.

"I never said that," I tell him. Refuse to look him in the eyes. Refuse to give him my attention. "Where do you live?"

"Answer my question, Robbie. Quid quo pro."

"Do you even know what that means?" I ask. My pen taps the blank page of my notebook, making little blue commas and dots all over the place.

"It means if you answer my question, I might tell you where I live." He smiles, loose and playful. This little shit thinks he's got me.

"I wanted to carry a gun," I tell him, but my little joke misfires and he's not amused. Or scared.

"So you wanted to carry a gun because you're afraid of death?" Joey pauses, looks around for Carolyn. "That's a little selfish, don't you think?"

"I answered your question, Joey. Your turn. Why were you on the bridge?"

"Did you ever have that feeling that you were destined for something greater?"

"Is that why you were there" On the pad I scribble quickly suicide? Make it look like I'm just doodling, so he's not so suspicious. "Were you destined to die on that bridge?"

"My dad kicked me out," he says. This boy's mind challenges me to change subjects quicker than I normally do. I have one primary goal: to get this kid to safety, but he's playing games.

"Was he being abusive?"

"No, he probably just doesn't like me so much right now."

"Did he hurt you?" I scribble down possible abuse. I write abusive father?

"No. I'm not some stereotype. My dad didn't hurt

me. He didn't abuse me. I'm not a victim of domestic violence of any kind."

"Okay then."

"If you have to know, he caught me in the house with someone else," says Joey. He winks at me.

"Like a sleepover?" I say. Try to be coy and indirect; if I don't make a big deal over it, neither will he.

"Really?" he says. He raises an eyebrow as he says, "I'm sixteen years old. What makes you think that I still have sleepovers?" He says sleepovers with air-quotes, adding to his annoyance factor.

"You're not in danger of hurting yourself further, are you?" I ask. I click the pen closed and look at him. I can't write this part down for the same reason I can't let him know that I'm taking detailed notes: The more I write, the more he'll think he's going to be some case study or mental patient. This will cause him to shut down. That's counterproductive.

"No, I'm not going to hurt myself."

"Good."

"How about you?" he says.

"'Scuse me?"

"Are you going to hurt yourself?" he says.

"Why would you ask that?"

"You're sad," he says. Joey's smile has disappeared,

replaced by a sobering smirk. "Aren't you?"

"We're not here to talk about me, okay?" My hand grabs the table on the sides, trying to keep them in once place, so I don't so something stupid. "We need to go."

"That's why you became a cop, wasn't it? That's why you love having a gun."

"Shut up. Now," I say nice and calm. I wish I had my gun right now.

"Your partner is the one who died."

My heart stops, freezes in place and cold sweats take over my chest and back.

"We're leaving," I say. Shuffling through my pockets, I realize I don't have any more change. "Dammit."

"Here," he says. Joey raises his hand up into the air and seconds later Carolyn comes back to our table.

"Check?"

"Yes, please," I say. Carolyn fingers through each of the receipts and leaves ours face-down on the white laminate tabletop and walks away without offering to take any cash right away.

Well, you seem to know so much about me, little shit. "So, what's your story?" I ask.

Joey sits back, crosses his arms. "So it's my turn?"

I nod.

"Dad caught me with someone when I was supposed to be home alone. At least I thought I was going to be home alone, or he wouldn't have been over," he says.

And before he can finish, I feel like I already know the rest of his story.

"Let me guess. You get caught with someone in your room. Father, furious that you ignored his orders, throws the other kid out of the house and then threatens you, who threatens to run away and disappear.

"Later, you get caught again, this time with someone else, and Father gets angry, threatens to beat you both, and you leave the house, never to be seen again," I say.

"You're a pretty good story-teller," says Joey. "But you're sort of right."

"Where do you live?" I ask. "We need to get you home."

"You won't find them there, I told you." He sits back and measures me and my reactions.

"Then where should I take you? The county courts?"

"Is it hard, you know, being gay on the force?" he says. Joey's head is tipped forward and to his left, leaning in like he's trying to listen in on some big secret.

"Don't know what you're talking about," I say.

"C'mon, really?" Joey leans in over the table. "It's okay, you can tell me, really."

"You're really crossing a line here."

"So you're not denying it," he says.

"My life is not up for discussion, Joey."

"But you won't answer my question," he says. "Why? Scared?"

"We're talking about you," I say.

"But we're not, really. We've been talking about you all this time," Joey says as he puts his hands up into the air again and Carolyn comes around the corner.

"Are y'all ready to pay?" she says.

I raise my hand up, my debit card tucked between my thumb and index finger, to flag down the waitress, and we pay. Joey seems abnormally attention-deficit as we exit the building, paying attention to everything that passes by us both on the street and in the air.

"Did you know that birds have different types of calls for different needs?" says Joey. He stands by the car and shields his eyes from the sun with his hand as he searches for birds to prove his point.

"Nope," I say. "Didn't care." The doors unlock with a muted click. "Get in."

Seatbelts click without me having to warn him. Good. He's learning.

"So where did you say this place was?"

"I didn't," he says.

"That was your cue to tell me right now so I can take you home."

"I already told you they aren't there," he says. He crosses his hands and watches the houses and trees go by the passenger side window.

"Then tell me now and we can track them down," I say. My eyes leave the road just long enough to watch him fiddle with the knobs on the radio and tap into the keyboard of my computer. "Stop that!" I slap his hand.

Joey shakes off the sting of the slap. "Ow," he says. "You're painful."

"I can do a lot worse if you keep this up."

"I believe you, I believe you," he says. He kisses the back of his hand.

"I don't know what game you are playing here, kid, but you're getting on my nerves, real quick." A blank spot on the side of the road is a perfect fit for a very necessary life lesson. "You're pushing my nerves, and I'm here to help, got that, Joey?"

"Yes, sir," he says, timid. I check his eyes, watch how fast his chest rises and falls. Not sure if he's being serious or not.

"I really hope so," I say. "If you're just going to get in the way, then I'd rather not struggle and just drop you off with the authorities."

Joey sighs, looks at me, his head tilted forward. "Fine." Another sigh. "1403 Well Drive."

"Now you're just messing with me," I say.

"Nope. You asked, I answered." I watch Joey's head turn toward me from the window in my peripheral vision. "You know it?"

FIVE

Joey's family home is larger than I expected, more than I remembered any of the houses being when I was here last about a year ago.

Holding the door open, I motion for Joey to get out of the passenger seat. He reluctantly gets out, shields his eyes from the sun above. "You sure you want to do this?" he says.

"I've been waiting to do this all day," I say. I grip his shoulder and nudge him forward. Joey drags his feet on the sidewalk, the muted rubber sound of shoe sole against hot cement announcing to me that he genuinely doesn't want to go home.

Before I decide to push the button, I search my pockets for my badge and check over Joey's body for any scratches or dirt. Gotta make him presentable, so his parents take him back.

"Ready?" he says.

I give him an awkward eye and think that was my line.

The doorbell sounds inside and a dog barks. By the high-pitched yelp, it's probably a small breed. Yorkie or poodle.

The door opens and the fresh scent of vanilla wafts outside. "Can I help you?" says a woman who pops her head around the corner of the door. She has a purple silk-polyester blouse that definitely leaves a lot to the imagination. She takes a step out from behind the door, and her bare feet coming out of her tan slacks tap on the floor. Out of nerves or fear, I can't tell. The woman's brown power bun, pulled tight behind her head, bobs up and down when she says, "Are you selling something?"

"I'm Detective Robert Lambert." Flash the badge and tuck it back away. "Is this your son?" I ask. I nudge Joey forward, and he smiles and nods his head.

She looks confused, frowns at me. "No, this isn't." She begins to smile. "Is this some kind of joke?" she says. "Did Melissa put you up to this?"

"No, ma'am," I say. "I found him out near the bridge, thought I'd take him home to his family."

"Well good luck with that, but his family isn't here."

"This is 1403 Well Drive?" I look at Joey, who bears a huge grin.

"Oh, this is the right place," she says. "But he doesn't live here," she says. Her finger points at Joey. "I'm sorry," she says and closes the door.

Joey turns to me, shrugs and begins his walk back to the car, "So how about some ice cream?"

I snatch his hood and yank him back to me. "Just one second." Joey's body snaps back to where I'm standing. "Where do you really live?"

"You asked, I told you," he says.

"That's not an answer." I can't help but to grit my teeth together. If I don't do something soon, I'm going to take my frustration out on this kid. "Where. Do. You. Really. Live?"

Joey points back at the house. "I lived here."

"Lived?"

"Well, apparently I don't live there anymore."

"That's it, you're going to cps."

"How about we get some ice cream first?" he says. Joey takes my hand, pulls it off of his hood and dusts himself off. "Seriously, I think there's a store somewhere around here." Joey's small pale hands point in various directions, trying to get his bearings. He peers down the street in one direction, then the second. "I think it's that way," he says, fingers pointing east toward downtown. What he's referring to is the old ice cream shop on the side of the street that closed down just ten years ago..

"It's not there anymore," I say. "Closed up shop a decade ago."

"No, seriously," he says. "Let's go. I'm sure it's right there." Joey walks to the side of the car, pulls on the handle and realizes that the locks are still in place. He looks at me and pulls on the handle once more, his expression asking me to open the door.

But something next door catches my eye. I walk to the next lawn over, and I remember this house. The white wooden panels and dark blue door. This was where I made my mistake.

"Officer?" Joey shouts at me. "Robbie! Over here!"

I ignore his calls. The window, up in the right corner on the second floor goes to the bedroom where the boy was shot and killed. I moved too slowly to save him. To save Brandon, my partner.

"Do you know these guys?" he says. Joey stands beside me, peering up at the window. "Wanna go in?"

he says.

"No, that would be breaking and entering."

"Only if we get caught," he says. Joey takes the initiative and takes the first few steps toward the front door. "C'mon."

"I'm a cop!" I shout to him as he walks away. "You're already caught."

Joey's hand grips the metal handle of the front door and pushes down. "It's open!" he announces.

I don't need this shit. Not now. I try not to make too much noise when I run up to the front door. Letting the homeowners know that we were there is not going to go over well, especially since I'm not in a uniform or anything.

"Shush!" Closing the door, I yank Joey's coat back to the car, nearly dragging him the entire way. "What has gotten into you?"

"You wanted to go in," he says.

"You just want to be arrested, don't you? What is your game?" I say.

"Game?"

It's then that a head pops out of the house—a woman's head—and she looks directly at me, through the window and at me, and looks like she's mouthing something when I start the car and drive off.

I choose not to fight this battle, thinking that Joey's

not going to believe me unless he sees it for himself.

As we're in the car, waiting for the light at Main and River to turn green, I glance at Joey's eyes, the way they watch the street, the people around, and then me. Over and over again. The way he acts, this boy seems like he might be new to this planet.

"Where did you say you're from again?" I ask.

"I've been from Saraday all my life," he says. He tucks a lock of blond hair back into his hood. "Just like you."

"When did I tell you I was from Saraday?" I ask.

"You look like you're from here." He smiles, which turns into a chuckle. "You just got that look about you."

I look at him, then the light just to watch it turn green. Before I can voice the syllables, Joey continues.

"You have that look like you're trying to get out. That stuck look that everyone has." Joey points out into the crowd, spots a red-haired young man walking down the street with his blue backpack thrown over his shoulder. "Like him." He points to another woman in a car next to us. "And her." He continues pointing. "And her. And him. And him."

"I get it," I say. "You're really annoying."

"I know," he says with a grin.

As the car carries us downtown toward to the old ice cream shop, the car's silence becomes a scream in my mind, an ice pick telling me to talk, to break the silence.

"I needed to stop having panic attacks about death," I say.

Joey's head snaps back to face me, raises an eyebrow.

"The answer to your question," I say. "I needed to stop having panic attacks about death."

He claps. "Ha! I knew it!"

"You're full of shit," I say. Eyes on the road. Try not to smack this kid right here.

"Oooh, you swore at a kid," he teases.

I find an empty parking spot in a nearby lot and lead Joey to the spot of the old ice cream parlor. We stop just outside, and Joey rests his small pale hands on the glass of the front door. The insides are dark with signs of construction abound.

"See?" I say. "Told you."

"That's ridiculous," he says. "I was just here, like yesterday."

"I highly doubt that," I say. I begin walking back to the car, and Joey, he rests his head on the door, staring into the darkness and sawdust and shelves that litter the floor. "C'mon," I say.

Joey says nothing. Instead, his forehead squeaks as he rubs it back and forth on the glass.

"You're going to leave a grease mark," I say. "Come on."

"No," he whispers, just loud enough for me to hear it, but not loud enough to be overtly defiant.

"Fine," I say. "Stay here."

No sounds and no footsteps mean that he might well be willing to stay there by himself. Maybe I really am done with this kid.

"Okay!" I shout out to him, one foot into my car. "I'll see you around!"

I wait a few more seconds and nothing. No sounds of the kid running.

I can't do this. "Aw, hell," I mutter. Around the corner is the boy, his head still against the wall, pushing with his hair-covered forehead. "Come on, I'll give you a ride to wherever your parents are," I say.

I look into the window and see the slight reflection, a foggy vague outline of Joey's head. Except, this head isn't the shape I remember.

"Joey?"

There's no movement, just a whining sound.

"Come on, it's not that bad," I say. "Maybe you were just somewhere else."

He still whines, ignoring my words, until I pull back on Joey's shoulder; try to show him that I'm not truly trying to be so distant.

When my eyes focus on what pops out at me, I take step back and see bright blue eyes, but brown hair coming from the jacket. The boy's face is chubby, at least ten pounds heavier than Joey's pale one.

"What the hell?" My hands work on reaction, and I push Joey into the brick wall on the side. "Who are you? Where is Joey?"

"I am Joey, Robbie," says the chubby face in Joey's face. This thing standing in front of me is Joey, but not Joey.

I reach for my sidearm, but realize I had it off all day today. I take a few steps back, my hands extended in front of me to keep this—this thing away from me.

"Where is Joey?" I demand. "Where is he?"

Cars pass by in increasing numbers. I'm making a scene as traffic is picking up. Must be the beginning of lunch hour.

"What the hell?" I say.

Joey—but not Joey—walks toward me and for the first time I can pull my eyes away from his ice-blue ones, away from the shortened brown curls that cover his forehead. What I can only see now are the pieces of light that come out of Joey-but-not-Joey's mouth when he talks. The light has warmth to it. I blink again and the light? It's sunlight coming from behind him.

"Come on," says the boy. "Stop playing around."

With every o sound, pieces of light shine through his mouth and I see a gunshot wound through his throat.

No. This isn't happening.

The boy walks closer to me, arms outstretched to me. It says, "Are you feeling okay?"

"Stay back. I swear to god, stay the fuck away from me," I shout at it.

"Fine, fine," he says. "I'll stay away from you."

The boy's cheeks and the skin around his eyes, they turn darker and redder. The color of frustration and anger.

With each step backward, my legs feel made of Jell-O. Every inch I take, they wobble more and more and the cold sweats, just like last time. They come back, chilling pinpricks on my back, itchy and wet.

"You're not real," I say.

"Sure, I am," the boy says. Joey-but-not-Joey pushes his hands forward and tries to grab me. Afraid of being touched, of being taken over by this thing, I reach up and pull my arms away from him, try to find some way to save myself.

Something kicks me in the heels, a rock or a part of the sidewalk pushed upward from normal wear and tear, I don't know. Gravity pulls me down, and I try to put my arms underneath me to catch my fall, keep my head from bouncing off the sidewalk.

The world feels jarred at first, and everything shakes for a split second. All I see is sky. Sky and clouds, and the top of buildings and fuzzy animals hiding in the clouds above.

"You took a big fall there, Robbie," says the boy and his hand grabs my knees to catch my attention.

"Stop!" I shout and hold up my hands to block my face, but golden hair, shining in the sunlight from behind him, illuminates Joey's head.

"Are you okay?" he asks. His hands extend out to me to grab my arms and pull me up. All five feet of him tries to yank me upwards until I shout at him to stop and let me do it myself.

"Where were you?" I ask.

"Right here, crazy," he says. Joey looks at the ground and points at an uneven spot of sidewalk. "That corner there tripped you when you were trying to run away from me."

"I wasn't running," I say. "Where was that other boy?"

Joey's face is blank, but I know he's judging me.

Play it off. Be in control.

"I'm sorry," I say. I check my hands for scratches or rocks buried in the skin. "I've been a little stressed out lately."

"Only a little?" asks the smart-ass.

"Glad to see you're back to normal," I mutter under my breath, but he still manages to hear it.

"Normal?" he asks. "What's normal anymore?"

SIX

"Watch this kid, will ya?" I say to Hernandez. Joey pulls his hood down over his eyes, waves over to Officer Hernandez and sits down a chair by her desk. "Thanks."

Mine is only a few steps away from her desk. What I don't tell them, however, is right now, I truly just want some privacy. Having the boy looking over my shoulder will be counterproductive.

"Hey, Nancy," I say over the phone. "Can we look up a previous owner for a house? 1401 Well Drive. That's right. Ya, I need to get some history for personal reasons. Thanks, dear. I'll hold."

"You do know you're not supposed to be on the job, right?" says Hernandez. She rests her ass on my desk, putting her hands near mine as she tries to peek over my desk, her body hunched backwards to accentuate her ass and hips.

She didn't get the memo.

"I'm just getting some research done. For the kid," I say, pointing my phone over there. As in, you need to be watching this boy, Hernandez kind of a point.

"Should I just lock him up? Save us both the trouble?" she smiles. She looks over in Joey's direction and winks.

"Do whatever," I say. "I don't care." On my desktop computer, I type in Joey and my fingers don't know where else to go. "Hey, kid!" Joey puts down a statue of a monkey thinking and looks in my direction. "What's your last name?" I ask.

"For what?" he screams back at me.

"For. For. For never mind," I say back. I click on South Carolina's database for missing persons, looking for a teenage boy by the name of Joey, if that is his real name.

A quick skim of the pages reveals that there's no one there who has his name. A second go through tells me that Joey probably isn't missing, or no one reported him.

Neither one would likely surprise me at the moment.

A little voice buzzes into my ear. "Hello? Yes, I'm still here," I say. "You're sure that's correct? Twenty-five years?" I scribble a few notes onto the pad of paper, the address 1403 Well Drive, 25 years, and Smithsons.

When I look up, I don't see anyone near the chair where I left Joey.

"Jesus H.," I groan and stand up. "I will duct tape you to the chair next time." Hernandez's desk is empty, too. No one there and no sign of where she went. "Hernandez?" I announce. "Joey?"

No one answers back. The rest of the office buzzes with busy police officers and phone calls for help. The boys in blue who share our office, they completely ignore me and my calls.

"Where the hell are you? Hernandez? Why the fuck did you let this boy wander?"

"Over here," a voice whispers to me. It's Joey, I'm sure of it. My feet carry me to the far corner of the office, following the source of the whispered clues.

That's where find Joey's feet propped up on the desk, his hands behind his head, and his generous smile across his pale face. "What took you so long?" he says.

"I should have cuffed you to the chair," I say. "Get up, you're not supposed to be here." I snap my finger and point in the general direction of my desk. "Hop to it."

I recognize the desk and the darkened spot on the walls where his posters and certificates were.

"What was this guy like?" he says.

"None of your goddamned business. Get out," I say.

"He must have been a nice guy," he says. "What happened to him?"

"How do you know it was a him?" If I can play stupid, get him out of there, he can't pull on my strings.

Joey catches on, winks, and says, "C'mon. Really?" Joey kicks his feet off the desk and goes through the drawers, damn near crawling into each of them as he peeks in and around the shelves.

"None of this is your business, Joey. Come on."

Joey stands up, goes to the bookshelf, a small one left behind when my partner died. He goes through the books, picks one out, and then flips through the pages.

"Do I have to count to ten?" I say.

Joey pauses in the book, looks at me through his blond bangs. "Do I look like I'm ten?"

Part out of frustration, part out of threat, I pull my handcuffs out of my pocket and stretch the chain out. "Know what these are?"

"Kinky," says Joey. "But at work? That's just poor taste."

I toss the cuffs at him. He barely catches them, and the sound of them jingling in his hands startles him. "Put these on." Joey pauses, looks at me, checking out each eye to see if I'm serious.

"Now." I draw my gun. "This is getting ridiculous. If I come near you, I'll kill you."

"You're awfully temperamental," he says. "Do they go on like this?" Joey holds his hands out, the bracelets almost nearly pressed up against his tiny wrists.

"Don't be stupid," I demand. I click the cuffs closed on each of his wrists. He responds with winces of pain. "Serves you right."

"Do I get to go to jail?" he says. "I've never been to jail before."

"No, you're not going to jail. You're going to sit next to me until we're ready to leave." Joey grudgingly drags as he follows. His arms hang low in front of him, acting as if the weight of the cuffs became too heavy for him. I say acting because we both know it is. He's just messing with me, and I don't know why I can't shake him.

"So what do we do now?" he says.

"Where do you really live?"

Joey pauses, scratches his nose with both of his

index fingers. "Are these things supposed to itch?" he says.

"Not your face. Where do you live?"

"I told you that already."

"You haven't been there before," I say. "That family has been there for the past twenty-five years at least."

"Ya, that makes about sense, I guess."

"Have you heard a single word I said?" We get back to my desk, and I point to a chair opposite mine. Joey follows directions and sits down, crosses his legs.

"Yup. Twenty-five years. That family," he pauses, looks upwards into his eye sockets. "I haven't been there. That about cover it?"

Hernandez appears around the corner holding two Styrofoam cups of steaming something. "Coffee?" she says.

"You know I cut down on my coffee," I say, and Hernandez ignores the comment, places the cup in front of Joey.

"Thanks, Jillian."

"Jillian?" I ask. Pointing at Hernandez, I say, "You left him to get him coffee? I said watch him."

"He's not a perp or anything, so I didn't think anything of it. You're not like babysitting him or anything, are you?" Hernandez eyes her coffee and nods at me with a look that asks if I want it.

The coffee is damn near white from all the creamer, and probably as sweet as syrup.

I wave it off with my left hand. "I needed you to keep an eye on this kid," I say. "He's needed for an investigation," I say.

"You're not supposed to be on any cases," she says. "Go home and rest. Drop him off to his parents or something."

"If only it were that easy," I say.

Both of us direct our eyes to Joey, who's sitting at the chair, leaning backwards and cupping the coffee in both of his handcuffed hands. He brings the rim of the coffee close to his mouth, then pulls it away as the steam licks at his face.

"Can I get some ice?" he says.

"No, you cannot." I grab my car keys and gun off the desk, and say, "Thanks anyway, Hernandez. I'll take it from here."

"You know, I can take the kid back home if you want. You go home and rest for a few days."

I'm tired of having people tell me that I need to relax. I'm tired of having everyone feel sorry for me. I'm just tired. Tired of everything. And this little shit isn't helping at all.

"C'mon," I say. I point to the door, and Joey's head

follows my fingertips.

"We going?" he says, rests the coffee on my desk.

"Yup, let's go."

"But what about my coffee?" he says.

"Leave it, it'll just stunt your growth anyway," I say.

SEVEN

"Can we stop and get more coffee?" he says. "That stuff was pretty good."

"We're not stopping anywhere, unless it's the hospital," I say.

"Is that a joke?" he says. "Oooh, you're going to kill me," he mocks, waves the handcuffed wrists in my face. "Big bad cop is going to handcuff me and kill me."

Keeping my hands on the wheel, eyes on the road, I try to have a serious conversation with him. "I've tried being nice, but you're just incorrigible."

"I can't even spell the word," he interjects, smiles at his own cleverness.

"I don't doubt it. Listen, I've had enough of all of this bullshit. You clearly don't want any help, but I can't just let you go, so we need to get you checked out, make sure you're okay."

"I'm feeling fine, thanks for asking," he says.

"That's not what I meant, and I need to hear it from a doctor, that's all."

"You don't believe lil old me?" he says. "I'm hurt."

"Not yet, but you will be if you keep it up."

Once we're at the hospital, I pull into the emergency room drop off and use the red light as permission to park wherever the hell I want. "Get out," I say.

"No."

And those words, they hit my brain like a mallet. "No?" I rub my eyes, try to concentrate and release tension. "You're not in a position to tell me no," I say.

Joey's face displays confusion as his eyes look from left to right, clearly searching for a clue. "But I just did."

I pull my gun on instinct, open the door and hold it against his head. "You're going to get out of this goddamned car if I have to drag you by your hippy hair."

"That's pretty fucked up, Robbie. All you had to

do was ask nicely." Joey's hands wave the barrel of the gun away from his face, and he says, "Excuse me." As I step aside Joey takes a step out and looks around. "Can I at least get these things off of me? Silver isn't my color."

"Just be happy I haven't shot you yet," I mutter under my breath, but still quiet enough so no one else here can hear me threaten a teenager.

"Oh, how the mighty have fallen," he says.

The doors open, and fresh sterile air blows in our face from above the electric sliding doors. I approach the desk, pulling out my badge from my pocket.

"I need to get a young boy checked out, found him outside," I tell her. Joey stands next to me, raises his cuffed hands in front of the nurse and waves with a friendly smile.

"Sure thing," she says. The nurse flips through a chart, pulls out a piece of paper and says to me, "Just one second." She gets up from behind the desk and goes into a backroom right behind her. The door swings open as a head pops in, looks at us, then goes back behind the door. More whispering.

Joey just stares at me. "So, how about that sports team?"

Roll my eyes, keep from hollering out and smacking him.

"We'll see you in the back," she says. We follow her back behind the doors and more people sit all along the sides of the wall on padded benches, holding bandages and ice packs against their skin. An African-American woman holds a stack of gauze against her forehead.

"Poor people," says Joey.

"Oh, now you have heart?" I say.

"I'm not all chaos and jokes, you know." Joey breaks from our line to the examining room and approaches the woman with the gauze against her eye. He rests his hand against the woman's head, bows his head, and whispers something incoherent.

The woman looks up at the boy, says, "Who are you?" and takes the gauze away from her head.

Joey simply smiles and puts his hand on her lap, saying, "Just remember that He loves you."

"Excuse me, ma'am," I say as I grab Joey's hood and drag him away from the woman. We turn the corner to the right and enter into one of the examining rooms. Tools of the trade line the walls in a plastic holster nailed to the wall. The cabinets are lined with hazardous stickers, and a white plastic box hangs from the wall, declaring that everything inside is "hazardous waste."

"So what are you guys looking for?" says Joey.

"Cut the crap." Pointing at the door, I ask, "What was that out there?"

"She needed hope," he says. "You saw her. She was beaten up pretty bad. Just helping her out a little bit."

"You can't go around laying hands on people and telling them that someone loves them," I say. "You're not a healer, and you're just going to give someone false hope if you catch the wrong person."

"But I caught you," he says.

"Just what the hell is that supposed to mean?"

I don't get an answer when the door opens, and a bald head with little white hairs on the sides pops his head inside. "Everything okay?" he says.

"That's what we're supposed to find out," I say. "I'm Detective Lambert." He takes my hand. "This is Joey," and Joey raises his hands as before, the handcuffs jingling.

"Sup?" he says.

"I need you to take a look at this boy. We found him outside, trying to—" and I pause. I can't tell them that he was trying to kill himself, or they'd try to lock him up for seventy-two hours. Can't have that. Not yet, anyway. "Trying to get into some trouble. Just needed to make sure he's okay before we drop him off to his parents."

"Well, we don't normally just do this here, and

now, detective, I'm sure you understand."

"I do, and you know, I'm really sorry about using my position like this." I pause, stare at the ground, looking at his shoes, watching Joey's feet kick the examination bed. "This just couldn't wait."

"Well, what am I looking for?" he says. "Is there anything in particular I should be looking for?"

"No, not that I know of," I say. "Just an overall check up, I guess."

"Does he have to stay in here?" says Joey. "I mean, I just barely met the guy."

The doctor looks at me, raises his eyebrows as if to ask the same question.

"Fair enough," I say. "I'll be outside."

The door clicks behind me, and I wish to God I never looked up. Room 14. Where he died. My heart takes a great hulking swan dive into my stomach, bobbing up and down like a Halloween apple.

"Can I help you?" asks a voice—a female voice— behind me.

"No, I'm fine." I don't turn around. Showing an emotion is not what I want to do right now. Cops aren't supposed to cry for no reason. Not appropriate for a detective in an emergency room. This is not an episode of er.

"Are you sure?" The voice goes a little softer,

kinder, gentler. "You look a little lost," she says.

"I'm fine, just waiting." I point to the door, shrug, and try to play it off as best I can.

The shoes—high heels from the sound—walk away from behind me without a further explanation and I can't help but to walk closer and closer to the door. No light coming from underneath the doorway.

I take care to make no noises when I turn the knob, just in case I'm not supposed to be doing any of this.

Inside is the bed, made up with a baby blue blanket and white sheets, tightly fitted and bed made up in typical hospital style. I let myself in and touch the bed as if by touching the bed I was somehow touching him. I know he's not there, but it's easy to say that maybe he's there in spirit.

I wish I believed in that crap.

Like a haunting memory, the beeps of the machines tick away Brandon's life. The crash cart squeaks as it bursts through the door, every bit as dramatic as you see on television. Every available nurse and doctor hovers around Brandon to keep him from dying from his gunshot wound.

The scene plays in my mind like a movie in slow motion: The heart rate monitor beeps slower, slower, until a long, steady beep sounds off into the hospital air. My head peers out of the room, shouting for help.

Please can someone come save him, please. Can anyone do anything. Please he's dying.

Hospital personnel floods the room, pushing me back into the corner, and I watch—forgetting to breathe—as people in blue and green scrubs cover all views of Brandon. My heart sinks Titanic-style, and begs to be saved.

"Clear!"

The deep, chest-beating thump of Brandon's body convulsing against the bed.

"Clear!"

With every convulsion of his body, my head shakes. I'm blinded by the bodies in the way, letting my imagination fill in the gaps, wishing I could block it all out.

After twenty minutes, it's all over. A short, but quick, nurse, long curly brown hair and deep green eyes, she takes my shoulders and escorts me out of the room. Tears blurred my vision and my throat was paralyzed. I couldn't swallow my fear and my sorrow. Couldn't speak a single word, no "I'm sorry" or "I love you."

The nurse sits me in a chair just outside in the hallway, gives me a paper cone of water. "I'm sorry for your loss," she says.

Anger isn't the right response, but it's the only one that makes sense to me. My legs collapse underneath me as I sit on the bed. My hands form tight fists, punching the pillow. Speaking in syllables, punching in staccato motions.

"Stupid."

Punch.

"Stupid."

Punch.

"Me."

Punch.

"Excuse me," says a voice behind me. Another nurse. This one male. "No one is supposed to be in here."

I wipe my eyes, take the time to catch my breath and fix the pillow in front of me.

The nurse says, "Sir?" only louder this time. "You're not supposed to be in here." I stand up, shielding my eyes by staring at the ground.

"I'm sorry," I say.

The nurse must be confused, vocal sounds trying to escape from his throat, but he doesn't know what sounds to make, what words to say. How often does one really run into a grown man crying in a hospital room? Finally, he manages to speak a solid sentence. "Are you okay?"

"Fine. Yes. Okay."

The man eyes me, searching for some sense of truth. I won't look him in the eyes. Shame controls everything.

When we exit the room, the nurse closes the door tight behind him, looks at me, then proceeds with the rest of his day down the hallway.

I lean my back up against the wall next to Room 12, where Joey is being checked out by the doctor.

I think I must be hearing things when I swear I hear a voice from Room 14. "Bullshit," I mutter under my breath, but the voice from Room 14 calls out again, this time in pain.

No one else in the hallway responds to the sound, the baying of pain or orgasmic pleasure, I'm not sure. No other nurses hint at hearing the sound. No one else slows down, look at the door, acknowledges the reality.

"I just left the room," I say to the imaginary voice. "You're not real. No one is in there."

And then someone raps on the door of Room 14 from inside.

My first reaction is to recount the symptoms of PTSD. Depression, check. Arousal reactions, check. Avoidance, check.

I'm certainly on my way.

The door clicks open, no moan, no other signs of

life, but my heart wants to jump out of my chest and run down the hall screaming for help.

I approach the door, putting my hand on the handle and pull slightly. However something like an invisible force keeps the door from closing completely. I look down below under the door and near the hinges. Nothing.

"Um, guys?" I say out to the nurses and busy office staff. "Something's wrong with the door."

I get the idea to let go of the handle and see what is pulling on the door.

But I swear, there was no one there a second ago.

The door swings open and slams loud against the wall.

Darkness in the room, lights off and no signs of life.

Imagining things in the middle of the day? These are signs of schizophrenia, not PTSD. Maybe things are worse than they thought. When I turn around at the sound of Room 12's door opening, Joey stands in front of me, waving and pulling up his jacket sleeves just up to his elbow.

"What's up?" he says.

"Nothing," I tell him. "What did the doctor say?"

The bald doctor comes out of the room and hands me a piece of paper. "Everything's fine," he says. "Clean bill of health."

Joey beams with pride.

"Great, so there's nothing wrong with him?"

"Have a great day," says the doc. He tucks his hands deep into his white coat pockets and walks away to the front office to gather more clipboards and their patients.

"You look spooked," says Joey.

"Ignore that," I say. "We need to get going."

"To where?" says Joey.

The car ride is silent on the way back to 1402 Well Drive until my cell phone rings. I command Joey to hand me the cell phone, and the caller ID causes my stomach to churn.

"Do me a favor and keep quiet," I say. Then, into the phone, "Hello?"

"What the hell do you think you're doing, Lambert?" says the phone. It's my boss, Frank. Joey's ears perk up, moving and leaning in toward me as Frank's voice gets louder.

"I'm just heading home, sir," I say, nice and calm.

"Bullshit," he shouts so hard through the phone that it vibrates the plastic piece over the receiver. "Don't lie to me, Lambert."

"Sir," I say, swallow some spit and look over at Joey, "I have no reason to lie to you."

"Then I guess we'll have to see about that, won't we?" Frank says.

"We'll have to make this fast, kid."

"You didn't even say where we were going, Robbie," says Joey. He looks out the window, at me, then back out the window. In the reflection of the window I swear I see him smiling at me. A toothy grin that makes me think something has gone awry. Maybe he knows something's wrong. With me or with him.

Or maybe it's epilepsy.

"Turn here," he says and points at the right corner.

"How do you do that?" I ask.

"Do what?"

"You know where we're going, don't you?" I say.

He gives me his trademark smile of his, the one that pisses me off. As a detective, I hate not knowing. "I have a pretty good guess, yes." Joey rolls down the window and sticks his head out. "The weather sure is nice this time of year."

It's tempting to roll the window up with his neck in the open space. Just be done with all of this, but when I put my finger on the button, I can't press it. My body refuses to do what I tell it to do.

"Don't worry," he says. "We're almost there."

"No, we're not," I say. Instead of turning right, I go left and shut off the blinker.

"What are you doing?" he says. Joey's voice rings through calm, collected. Each syllable of his questions probes my brain, a jaws-of-life kind of questioning, drawing out the answers before I can even hide them.

"Finding a place to hide your body," I say. "You're getting on my nerves."

The words just come rushing out of my mouth, so they must be truths. I feel Joey kicking around in my head, my brain not answering to me but to him and forcing me to say whatever he needs to hear.

"How are you doing this?" I ask. "Why can't I…"

"Lie to me?" he says. "Because I don't want you to." Joey crosses his arms across his chest and puffs up his chest to look bigger in the seat next to me. "Secrets don't make friends, Robbie."

"You know, that's really funny coming from you."

"I'm not keeping any secrets, Robbie. I'm just not telling you anything because you didn't ask the right questions."

And my mind goes blank. I'm on autopilot driving three blocks down the road to a two story red brick school that sits just on the eastern borders of the town of Saraday. "We're here."

"We're going to school?" he says and unbuckles

the seatbelt. "Are we going in for show-and-tell?" He laughs. "Can't I at least tell them that you're an insurance adjustor? I mean, you didn't even bring your gun."

I pull the gun from the back of my pants and show it to him. I unload the clip, show him it's loaded and click it back in place.

"Now we're talking," he says.

We're greeted at the front office by a Hispanic lady, short and stocky with an ear-to-ear smile that welcomes and frightens at the same time. "Hello!" she says. "What can I do for you?"

"Hi, I'm Detective Lambert. Do you recognize this child?" I say. Joey grunts as his chest hits the desk as I shove him into it. "He's out of school today, and I thought maybe you'd be missing someone."

The woman looks at Joey, squints and shakes her head. "Mmm. No. Doesn't look familiar," she says. She shakes her head at me, then to him. "What's your name, dear, maybe we can go find him."

"Trevor," he says.

My grip on his jacket tightens and my fingers feel like they are going numb. He's either telling the truth now or jerking both of us around.

"Trevor what, dear?" The front desk lady types a few words into the computer and waits.

"Trevor Parker."

The lady's fingers hunt and peck the word Parker, and she clicks something with the mouse. Joey smiles at me and pushes my hand off his jacket hood and presses it clean, straightening it out.

"Anything?" I ask. I lean over the desk to see the computer screen.

"I'm sorry, sir," she says, covers the screen with her arm. "This isn't for the public." She turns the flat screen monitor ten degrees to the left and squints at the picture. "I don't think your joke is too funny."

"What joke?" I ask. I grip Joey's hood with my left and hold him tight against the desk. "What joke is she talking about, Trevor?"

"His name isn't Trevor. At least he's not the Trevor Parker we know." The lady points at my hand and Joey's face turning red. "I think you're hurting him."

"He'll be fine. I'm a cop." Not that those two things have anything to do with each other. "What's the joke?"

The lady raises her index finger to tell us to wait here and disappears around the corner and into an office down the hall. The door closes and then reopens almost instantly. While the commotion is going on, I take a chance to peek around the monitor to see just who Trevor Parker actually is.

"What the hell did you do?" I ask him. "Who's Trevor?"

A tall bald man, overweight with a tie that stops just before where his bellybutton would be, approaches us and gestures—open palmed—to the door of his office. "I'm Jon Stedarow, the principal here. Please follow me."

I follow him into the office and Joey stands at the entrance. I shoot him a glance that tells him he's in trouble. Even over thirty, I don't like being in the principal's office.

"I need to see your badge before we continue this conversation," he says.

"When do I get a badge?" says Joey.

"Stand outside," I say. Joey grimaces at me and holds it, refusing to go anywhere. I point at the desk. "Now!"

Joey leaves the room, closes the door and leans backwards into the glass window that points out into the hallway. Joey's greasy blond hair leaves faint translucent streaks as he waves his head back and forth across the glass.

"I'll have him wash that, I swear," I say.

The principal dismisses it with a wave of his hand and sits on the corner of his desk. "If you're with the Saraday Police Department, then you must know who

Trevor Parker is."

Nothing rings a bell, but my palms turn sweaty. I shrug.

"He was the boy who was killed late last month by his abductor," says the man. He puts his hands on his lap and presses down to support his shoulder weight. "What exactly do they tell you guys down there?"

Fuck. Fuck. Fuck. Fuck.

"That's classified," I say. Not true, exactly, but no one ever argues with this point. "Can I sit down?" The question was more of a formality as I take the chair anyway and sit, covering my face with my hands. My shoulders and back feel cold and clammy. Everything else burns hot and I can't breathe.

"Are you okay?" he says. Jon stands up and tries to look me in the eyes, despite my covering them. "Do you maybe want me to get you some water?" he asks. "We can get you some water."

I hold my hand up, shake my head no.

"You're sure?" he says.

I nod. "I'm okay. I'm fine." My stomach does jumping jacks in my belly and my heart hurts, and gasps for breath, winded like a marathon runner. "Yes, I'm fine." Panic attack? "Just asthma," I say.

Breathe, Robert.

Breathe.

Jon pauses. I can nearly hear him evaluate whether to call Nine-one-one or keep going. "Then, um, then you know that that child is not Trevor Parker."

"He told me his name is Joey." My hands wipe the sweat off my brow and I look up at him, squinting from the fluorescent lights. I don't remember them being this bright a few seconds ago. "He was found at a bridge on the outskirts of town." My words come out slow and methodical as I try to get my tongue to sound coherent and form words that sound and feel right. "I thought maybe he might be missing school, or at least this would be a safe place for him to be. You know, keep him out of trouble and whatnot."

"We'd take him for sure, detective, but we can't. He's not enrolled, and the person he says he is appears to be dead."

Of course, because nothing today has gone the way I wanted it to. "Nothing you can do?" I ask.

"Nothing I can do."

I make a slow reach for the door, saying, "Thanks for your time." As the door cracks open, Joey rushes to the front door, a forgotten puppy waiting for his master. "Are you sure you haven't seen him around anywhere?" I ask.

"I visit every classroom at least once a week. I have not seen that boy here. Maybe he's from Columbia or

Charleston." The principal waves and barely fits in the stuffed black chair at his desk.

I close the door to notice that Joey isn't standing where I told him to be.

"I will kill this kid," I say unapologetic even with these school staff around me. "It's okay," I tell the principal. "I'm a detective." The door closes behind me.

If I were a delinquent, where would I hide?

A student bumps into my side, not watching where he's going. "'Scuse me," he says. The boy, probably about fourteen or fifteen pseudo-smiles at me, pushing his cheeks back but not actually trying to smile and walks past me. His own black hoodie flaps behind him as he walks in long, bouncy strides. The boy's jet black hair reflects a dyed blue tint in the fluorescent lighting. Black jeans. Black shoes. All nearly identical to Joey's clothing and I realize that I'm in trouble. Needle in a haystack trouble.

I don't ask for permission when I just walk down the hallway to the back teacher's lounge and poke my head into the window. Since Joey isn't going to class here, he could be hiding anywhere. He's a quick little shit with quiet steps that make it too easy for him to sneak up on anyone or anywhere.

My steps slow down to feel the air around me

and figure out any scents that might tip me off that he's around here. It's when I slow down that I realize that interstates and school hallways have the same problems: congestion. Something bumps into my back and his hand grabs my ass as a way to stop.

"Sorry, sir," he says.

"Oh, no, I'm sorry," I say and try to turn around, but close walls keep me from going in more than one direction at a time. When I turn around, it's the same boy with blue-black hair and navy black hoodie. The baby-blue painted metal door shuts behind him as he leaves the building, presumably to go to classes.

This seemed like as good a place as any to start.

The hefty Hispanic lady from the front counter hands me a map of the school after I explain that I need to survey the area. She doesn't ask where my "son" is and why I need the map. Safety issue, but no time to discuss it.

From where I'm standing, there is a hallway of 300-numbered classrooms. I'll start there and circle around.

If I had to take my guess, the school was over a hundred years old, built by brick in a time when they still cared about how sturdy a building should be. South Carolina isn't prone to earthquakes—not big ones anyway—but hurricanes are a threat nearly six months out of the year. It's always important to have strong buildings that can serve as shelters if the storms get too strong for the regular houses to handle.

The sun's rays warm my skin but have essentially kicked me in the eyes. Everything is white and pale, and for a brief second, I'm not sure which direction I'm turning.

"Where ya going, Robbie?"

"Joey!" I reach out into the air to grab Joey. "Stay there." Nothing anywhere. My eyes start to hurt, and there in the sunlight, everything begins to dim, more visible.

"Robbie?" says a shadow, and what stands before me is dark haired Joey-but-not-Joey again.

"Who are you?" I say. A couple leans quietly and carefully against the wall and begins making out. They don't see me or don't care. They certainly don't see this dark angel in front of me.

"I'm the Ghost of Cases Past, silly," he says. His eyes go white, flashing ice-blue irises in between syllables. "Any more questions?"

"Where is Joey?"

"Joey's not here right now. Please leave a message."

I'm partly surprised that I'm able to grab Joey-but-not-Joey's clothing with my fists and haul him into the next room. It happens to be a bathroom, light blue tiles and the smell of urinal cakes creeping out below the door. "Get in here!"

We swing around without resistance. I honestly expected this dark-haired son of a bitch to go limp or put up a little bit of a fight, but he doesn't.

"I'm tired of this shit," I say. "You're not real. You're not real. You're not real!"

"Then why can I do this?" he says and holds up his hands with just the fingertips sticking out of his raven black hoodie sleeves. His eyes direct mine to look at his fingers on the left hand, and he snaps them loud. The sound echoes off the walls, getting bigger with each bounce off the tiles until it hits my ears and rings my head. Vibrations so hard, they shake my jaw, and I clench together, squeeze my eyes shut and cover my ears to keep from going insane.

"What the?" I ask, but with opened eyes, I'm transported to the hallway, a familiar hallway.

And though I know it's not him, I see Brandon putting his ear against a door in a dark cherry-wood hallway. I recognize this hallway. I know this hallway. This is the hallway that led me to the tenth level of Hell.

"Not real," I say. "Not real. Not. Real."

"Clear," says Brandon.

"Dammit, Joey. It's not real."

"My name isn't Joey," teases the voice from in front of me. "What are you doing?" says Brandon. "I need you to focus. You'll fuck this up."

"It's already fucked up, Brandon. We can do this differently."

"Differently?" he says. My boyfriend searches my eyes for a meaning of the word differently and gives up. "Go sit in the car. I'll finish this myself."

"You're going to get yourself killed!" I pull on Brandon's shirt, and after I've pulled away I wish I could go back and rub his shoulder again, to relish the threads under my fingertips.

"Not if you don't keep down!" says Brandon. He points his gun toward the door and aims downward at the god-awful blue carpet, creeps forward. "Get out of here."

A jiggle of the handle makes both of us stop what we're doing and stare at the front door. Incandescent light escapes and instead of Brandon standing in front of me, the dark-haired angel stands before me, facing me.

He smiles, his blue eyes capture mine. And though these thoughts go through my mind, my body doesn't want to do anything. Nothing but watch. Nothing but blink.

"Wake up, Robbie." It's Joey, standing above me.

Which means that I'm essentially on the floor. Explains the cold feeling against the small of my back where my shirt must have been pulled up.

"What?" My voice feels cloudy and rough as the words try to scrape against my throat to be free.

"You fell down." Joey extends his hands in a gesture to help. "Something must have got you."

"I'm too old for this shit," I say.

"Too old?" Joey says. He places his hands on his hips, tilts his head and measures. "What? Like 26?"

"You're not getting anything from me."

A group of kids makes me the center of their huddled up circle. "Dude, you okay?" says the brave little boy in the front.

"Yup." Dust off the pants, try to act natural. "Just fine, thanks."

"Dude, who's Brandon?"

The warm blood rushing to my face. "I, um. Don't know." Play it off. Play it cool.

"Good enough for me," says Joey. "C'mon," he says. "Let's go."

"I'm fine." I yank my hand out of Joey's. "Really, I'm good."

"You're freaking out a lot lately. Are you sure you're okay, detective?"

My hands want to wrap around this little boy's pale

neck and squeeze until his head pops like a champagne cork.

"Are you really going to ask me this?"

"I just wanted to make sure you're okay," he says. His words say that he's concerned, but his face looks cold, still. Confused isn't the right emotion, but it's the closest I've got. "Just okay?" I have to clench my fists as hard as possible to keep from grabbing him by the face and squeezing.

"You're freaking me out, Robbie."

I have to look away because if I don't, I'll burst out into laughter or scream out loud. I'm not sure which. "We're done here. You're old enough to be on your own."

"You can't do that!" he screams at me. "You aren't allowed to just leave."

"Sure I am," I say. "Just watch me leave now." I make two steps toward the main hallway, to the front office. "See this?" Two more steps. "Look at me leaving." Two more steps. "And here I go."

My shoes squeak down the hallway amongst the slamming of lockers and the kids not trying to get to class on time.

And in my head, there's this thing talking to me, telling me to go back. Go grab Joey and get out of here.

But I ignore it, though the voice scratches at the

bony walls of my head.

"Leave me alone, Joey," I say.

He comes running through the crowd, trying to wave to me. The sounds of the girls and boys screaming, offended, by Joey's lack of compassion and who gives a shit as he rushes through them to get to me.

I keep stomping, trying not to turn around and see just how close he may be to me, once I get outside. My mind itches with the thought that I'm just leaving him in a school he doesn't belong to. Did I seriously want to leave him in a place even though I'm a police officer? Was this maybe the wrong thing to do?

"I don't care," I tell myself because certainly no one else quite listens. "Fuck this. Fuck you, Joey."

I keep talking to myself, to shut out the voices and the itching from the insides of my head, straight through the main office. The staff looks at me cautious through the corners of their eyes. "Did they just let this crazy man wander through their halls?" they probably wonder.

I extend a magnificent middle finger to the front of the school and drive off, pulling back slowly at first, then gunning it as I get to the bus circle and flip on my red light to get the hell out of there.

EIGHT

At the light of Broadway and Wilmot, I almost hit Joey with my car. There he lie, sprawled out in a snow angel formation, ready to be completely run over when I get out of my car and drag him off to the side of the parking lot.

"You're an idiot," I say. The red lights from my rooftop illuminate Joey's pale cheeks, going red-white-red over and over again. His eyes, still sky blue, look at me in hope and despair at the same time "I told you to get lost."

"You told me you were done with me," he says. He wipes his nose, looks to see if it's bleeding. "I never said that I was done with you."

"See?" I say. My hands release his and I turn around to walk away back to my car. "See you later."

"I said I wasn't done with you!" he shouts back at me. Cars stop in the middle of the street as I walk from the sidewalk to the driver's side of my car and open the door.

I bite my tongue, careful to not say anything to keep this damn conversation going on again.

Just how he got there so fast is beyond me. Why he's stalking me, I can't tell you. Nothing makes sense anymore, and I don't want to go home. I can't go home because I still have Brandon's stuff there.

And though the rest of the street honks at me like I'm the asshole for almost hitting a kid in the street who shouldn't have been there, I sit in the seat anyway and stare into the horizon. The sun is ready to begin setting over the tops of the pine and palm trees that line the streets. The buildings twinkle as they reflect God's flashlight back on us ants. And my mind? I don't know where it is, but it sure as hell isn't here in the street with Joey waving at me.

"I said I'm not done with you," screams Joey, somehow, over the honking of the pissed off drivers around me. "You get your ass back here, mister."

I ignore him. I ignore him because—like stray

pets, and ugly people—if you respond to them, feed into the behavior, he'll just keep coming and coming and coming.

Joey's right foot steps into the street and a car drives by, nearly hitting him again.

"Are you fucking crazy?" I say, but not loud enough to penetrate the chaotic atmosphere of this traffic stop.

Joey doesn't look left or right. He looks straight at me, pissed off, and keeps taking large steps and scowling at me through his hood, head pointed down, but eyes straight at me. He doesn't answer my request.

I guess by stomping at me and trying to get himself killed, it seems, he's already answering my question.

And I can't do it. I can't just let him stand there and get killed while he's trying to get to me. People are watching, my lights are flashing, I'm already identified as a police officer. The last thing I need to do is get caught killing some kid in the middle of the street.

"Get your ass over here!" I shout. I hold out my hand like my old days as a traffic cop. This brings back memories as I stop some cars, arms extended and palms up to halt both sides of the street. "Get in the car."

When I blink, there is no Joey. I blink again, rub my eyes and prepare for more dark-haired boys harassing me and speaking in riddles.

"Joey?"

"Over here," he says from behind me. In my car, he's buckled, ready to go. "Come on," he says, waves to me to get into the car. "You'll get yourself killed."

It's tempting to pull the gun and just shoot him in my car, but again, I'm in public.

"Just how did you get over here?" I ask. Joey fiddles with his blond hair in the mirror of the passenger side visor. He shuffles it with his right hand, then left hand, then messes it up and shakes his head to let everything fall into place naturally.

"I followed you," he says.

"Yes, that was the obvious result." Urge to kill rising. Rising. "How did you get over here so fast?"

"I walked."

"No more games, Joey. No more riddles!" My right foot presses deeper into the accelerator, a visual cue to Joey to let him know that I'm starting to mean business.

"Fine, fine, fine. But you won't believe me."

"Try me. I've been a homicide detective and worked in the juvenile system. I've seen a lot."

"I'm not real."

"You're sitting in my car, you can move my visor. You can buckle yourself in. If you aren't real, how is all of that really happening?"

"It's happening because I make it happen," he says.

"But you're not real," I say partially to myself, partially to him. "I need coffee."

"Oh! Coffee!" he squeals. "I love coffee." He flips his hood up over his hair, tucks in the locks on the side. "Can we go get some?"

"So you're not real, but you love coffee?" And the thought that I'm being punished enters my mind, runs around for a little bit and escapes before I can take it too seriously.

"Sure, we can get coffee. There's a Starbucks right here."

We pull into the parking lot and get out. I keep the gun in the back of my pants, held tight by the belt in case this "imaginary boy" tries to anything stupid. In my list of things that are wrong with this boy, I didn't ever think to take delusional or schizophrenic. Maybe I brought him to the wrong doctor.

"What do you want?" I ask.

Joey stares at the menu and the chalk drawings advertising a new hazelnut cream coffee, and he scratches his head. "We didn't have coffee like this when I was growing up."

"One Frappuccino, coming up," I say.

"Is that good?" he says.

The woman at the counter adjusts her green apron across her breasts and smiles at me. She's at least twenty-one, hair curled up into a bun and held tight with a strategically placed pen. "Can I help you fine gentlemen?"

"So you can actually see this young boy?" I say.

The barista—Cassandra by her nametag—cocks her head to the side, confused.

"Bad joke," I say and dismiss it with a wave of my hand. "I'll have a venti mocha, iced. He'll have a hazelnut cream frappuccino. Grande."

Cassandra takes my money and somehow must think that I run a cult or something. Her eyes narrow as she turns around and squeezes a few pumps of a thin chocolate sauce into the bottom of an clear plastic cup.

Joey stares at the different bags of coffee and the bright silver and white packaging. "Are you sure this is still coffee?" he says. "I thought all coffee was dark?"

"It is dark in color, yes."

"But then why is this blonde?" he says. "Does it have hair?"

"Are you serious, kid?" Take a deep breath. Breathe in calm, breathe out frustration. "If you're messing with me, Joey, I'll leave you here."

"You still don't believe me, do you?"

"That obvious?"

Cassandra shouts out our orders, and I hand the ice cold plastic cup to Joey. "Here, try this."

His forehead nearly releases a vein, he's straining so hard to suck up the thick mixture into his mouth. "You did this on purpose," he says.

I can't help but to laugh. "No, they're usually a little thick. Let it sit, it'll melt a little."

Joey doesn't listen, instead sucking in the straw harder and harder, his face turning red, then purple.

"And don't forget to breathe."

"I'm not supposed to tell you this," he announces as we leave the coffee shop and get back to the car. He buckles himself in and looks at me with all seriousness. "I'm here to save you."

"Save me?" I say, smiling. This is rich. "You're the one jumping from a bridge and I'm the one that needs saving."

The ignition starts and I turn around to check for on-coming traffic for me to back out, but Joey grabs my face by my cheeks with both hands and squeezes. "I'm serious," he says. "And this coffee is really, really good."

"Joey, are you on any kind of medication?" I ask.

He thinks for a minute, then shakes his head. "Nope, can't think of anything."

More and more of this seems out of place and

hard to get hold of. "Okay," I say after a heavy sigh. "I'll bite."

Joey says nothing, looks at me the way a dog looks at you when you get naked in the bathroom.

"Go on with your story," I say.

"I'm here to save you, and I'm a ghost."

"So you're crazy with illusions of grandeur."

"I'm not crazy, and I don't know what that last part even means," he says. "So I can't have that." He sighs, rubs his hand through his hair and looks directly into my eyes. "I can see that you need help, detective. I'm here to help you because you helped me."

"And just what kind of help do I need?" I ask. "What do you think you can do for me? What can you possibly do for me that all of these other people can't do?"

"See that?" he says. He points to me, to my face. "That? That was anger."

"No shit, Sherlock. You've been chasing me down, feeding me bullshit about needing to help me, lying about where you live and where you're going. I think I deserve to be a little bit angry."

"I'm not lying," he says. His eyes wander the insides of the car cabin, looking for a clue or some way to explain what he's needs to say. "You know what?" he says. "Drive."

"No." I slam my hands on the steering wheel, so I don't hit anything else. "Hell no. We aren't going anywhere until you tell me what the fuck is going on."

"You swear a lot."

I bite my lip so hard I taste the iron taste of pennies.

He touches my leg, squeezes. "I'm sorry about that." Joey releases his hand and places it safely in his own lap. "Sorry," he says. He tries to pat my leg but stops what he's doing the minute he catches my glance. "Right."

I can't help but sigh. "Where are we going?"

"We're going to go to the house," he says.

"The house?"

"You know which one," he says. Joey points to the front glass, directly in front of us. "Go."

"And we're doing this because?"

"You wouldn't believe me if I told you," he says.

I don't immediately recognize the house when I arrive. The driveway carries stains of cars past, oil and pink liquids that was probably radiator fluid. Old cars might mean poorer families, or the father thought he was a handy man. Maybe.

Not where I wanted to be, but pretty much where

I thought he was leading me.

"Now you take my lead," he says. Joey's steps are light and quick as he covers space over the sidewalk. I say cover space because I'm not entirely certain he's walking, but moving effortlessly through space.

I blink, stare at his feet once more and there they are: sneakers, pant legs, walking, moving, creasing with every step.

I'm about ready to say something about his feet when I notice that he's inside already without any mention of knocking or asking who's home.

"Are you fucking stupid?" I say. Trouble comes from stupid actions, so I grab my gun and my badge just in case someone decides that they want to call Joey out on his bullshit.

Once I get inside, I'm immediately taken aback by the décor of the house. It's been changed in the past few weeks, I'd say. The house looks more homey, green furniture and blue paintings on the walls of houses and people and pets.

"Joey?" I ask.

My first few steps crunch the threads of freshly laid carpet. My eyes spot small threads of cardboard on the floor, nearby where the furniture looks to have been assembled. Definitely, the realtor spent some money to get rid of the murder vibe in here. Pray and hope the potential buyers didn't read the local newspapers before they agreed to see the layout.

"Joey?"

My first instinct is to go to the kitchen, with black new appliances and a toaster that's more high tech than the computer in my office den. I wonder what they're selling this place for. Maybe I'll get a "first responder's discount"?

"Joey?" I whisper. No response. "Dammit, where are you?"

The fact that I can hear the carpet crunching under my feet means that no one is home, and for once something seems to have gone right since I met this kid.

I pick up the steps and check the other side of the house. A room that looks set up to be an intended office. Nothing special here and no Joey.

I move upstairs, step by step, listening for which direction to go. At the top of the stairs, I'm met with the a large wooden bookshelf, carved flowers in the side and just two books and a flower vase with a lonely violet. Ya, that's realistic. I always have bookshelves for my two books.

"Joey?"

Still no response.

Someone looks to have left the first door on the

left cracked open, so I tap the door open with my finger and take a peek. The realtor's choice for this bedroom is a girl's bedroom. Smart, I guess. Pink and purples blind you at every glance, so I close the door and thank God that I don't have a little girl.

Underneath the door on the right, a shadow moves from left to right, so I rush to that door and poke it open. It, too, swings open quickly, but stops at a forty-five degree angle. I peek around the corner, and nothing's here.

"Tell me what you want from here," I say.

Nothing inside, no sign of Joey.

"This is getting ridiculous," I sigh. "Get out here now."

When I'm able to look at the rest of the room, I notice that the realtor suggests that this be the parent's master bedroom. That's not what this was when I first got here. Images enter my brain, the way the light comes in through the horizontal blinds and sheds the thin rays of light on the bedspread, everything comes back to me in slow trickles.

This was a case where things went from bad to worse while I was here.

"What are you doing here?" I say.

Turning around, I grab my gun and point it first.

Behind me is Joey. "Tag!" he says, extends his

hand and taps my shoulder. "You're it!"

Urge to kill rising.

"You need to calm down," he says. Joey rests on the bed and stretches out, falling backwards and bouncing on the what is probably a brand new mattress. "So, tell me about what happened here," he says.

"None of your business," I say. The gun goes back into my back belt in the small of my back. "We're leaving."

"We're not going anywhere," he says. "We need to talk."

"We're not talking about this," I say. "Not here, not now."

"Robbie, you need to meet me half way if we're going to get through this."

"There is no this to get through!" I scream at him. "Nothing!"

"And that," he says, pulling himself up in a sit-up, pointing at my face, "that was frustration."

"It's not frustration," I say.

"How are we supposed to be friends if you're going to keep lying to me, Robbie?"

"We were never friends."

And then silence, an awkward silence where I feel like I should say sorry, but I can't. He doesn't deserve it.

Then, underneath us, I hear a door open and slam shut.

"Did you know someone is supposed to be home?" he says.

"You took me here," I say. I grab my badge in my left hand, gun in my right and hold them in front of me. "Go," I say, nodding to the front door.

"Sorry," he says. "No can do."

I open the door with the thumb and index finger of my left hand and out front lies a little girl clutching herself across her chest, fetal position. Crying and dress pulled up over her waist. The girl is eight years old. Her name is Sally Evans. She was the second child abuse victim I came across, the first of whom seriously affected me.

I lose track of time, space, location. My feet move on instinct, following the happenings. I kneel down and touch the girl's dress and pull it down around her legs, give her some dignity.

"Stop!" she screams and scratches at me. "Stay away!" Her nails draw blood from my wrist, droplets form at the skin.

"It's okay," I say. I hold the badge in front of her, and she looks, blinks, and then covers her head, crying.

"I'm so sorry," she says.

"It's okay." I grab her shoulders, try to pull her

up and to safety outside. She'll be safe there where someone can keep an eye on her. "Come on, dear."

"No!" she screams in a nearly glass-shattering scream and scratches at me again. Her nails tear at my skin, and a needle-thin stream of blood trickles down the sides of my thumb.

"I'll be right back," I say. I have the faint thought that she's not real, that something's wrong here, but like a movie, I watch myself act out what I'm supposed to do.

My steps carry me to the next bedroom to the left of this one. A white door, closed tight and shadows moving underneath, illuminated from the sunlight outside.

"Police!" I say. My gun remains pointed down, but directly in front of me. "Is everything okay?" I ask.

No answer, so I put my ear to the door. Stupid move.

Inside, gasps and moans, muffled through something other than the door. "Sir?" I ask. "Ma'am?"

Nothing.

I take my left hand, right hand held in front of me, to open the door and kick it open in a shock-and-awe manner.

A woman, short blond hair, her hands duct-taped to the bedposts, looks at me, her eyes wide. A cry for help and a muffled scream. The man who's plowing her doesn't notice me. Sweat reflects the sunlight into my eyes as it trickles from his balding head down the sides, behind his ears and down his shoulders. He grunts a disgusting noise each time he thrusts into her pelvis. As he finishes his thrust, she screams, moans, grunts into the thin pillow pressed and duct taped around the lower part of her mouth. His left hand moves down to the mattress to support his weight while his right covers her mouth.

"Shh," he says.

My hands follow the lines his body makes from right hand to his hairy feet on the floor, and I get all the permission I need to interrupt and lose my self-control.

A girl's panties. The girl from outside, small white panties with pink outlines where the seams were sown around the legs and waistband.

A bullet from my gun finds the man's brain, and he drops to the floor, still hard and sweating and dripping onto the carpet.

"Nice shot," says Joey. He leans against the wall between the bedrooms in the hallway, golf-clapping my shot with two fingers. "How does that feel?"

Sweat drops into my eyes and mouth, and wiping it out of my eyes just makes them more irritated. "What the hell is this?"

Turning my head to the left, there is no naked man. No woman tied to the bed. No duct tape. No hard on.

"What was that?" I say. I wipe my forehead with my sleeve, wipe that sleeve on my pants leg.

"That was therapy," he says.

I'm in the car before I can ask any further questions, give this kid too much power, and get myself into another shooting accident. Joey stands at the front door waving at me as I pull out the driveway. I announce to the inside of the car and anything that could be listening to me that "This is bullshit" and I drive off about as quickly as my shitty little car will let me.

At every stoplight, my eyes survey the area, searching for Joey, for black hoodies, for sneakers and blue jeans that might jump out into the street out of nowhere.

I get so far as to make it home when I pause in the car. My hand turns off the ignition, but I freeze, staring at the intricacies and craftsmanship of black plastic end of the key. Not for any particular deep meaning, not for details and inspiration. I stare because the key to find meaning in something is to lose focus. To understand, sometimes you need to see the forest for the trees. This key needs to be my forest.

The edges of the key are chipped into gray gashes from when I've dropped the keys too many times when I get home. The silver H on the wide end of the key is faded, and the silver painting nearly scraped off altogether.

My mind wanders to the shooting, the feeling of my fingers against the trigger, squeezing. I remember all of these, but I don't remember thinking, "I need to shoot this bastard." Nothing in my recent memory tells me that I needed to end his life, that he deserved to die.

That girl ended up in a foster family after I had rescued her nearly three years ago. Her neighbor had been raping her nearly every week for at least six months when the teacher announced that Sally had issues with going to the bathroom, with getting help when she had to pee. She was hesitant to be around men and refused to play with the boys. At times, she showed her underwear to the boys and laughed when she wanted attention.

These are the things that happen when you don't know you're being raped. You just know that it isn't good.

The mother killed herself a month after Sally was

taken away from her. I attended the funeral but didn't bring flowers. I didn't know what to do or say. I was responsible for taking her daughter away from her, the reason why she killed herself.

I couldn't say sorry to a woman who did nothing to protect her daughter from a monster.

Her suicide letter blamed her neighbors and blamed God for not saving her daughter from Satan. She blamed herself for not being able to handle the pain and told Sally that it wasn't her fault. None of this was.

Then she put an air bubble into her veins with a syringe and dropped to the floor in less than a second. The needle held still in her veins as she dropped to the carpet.

Thing is, I bought into the "blame the mother" mentality. No one deserves to see that kind of pain, especially a little eight-year-old girl.

My feet feel heavy, encased in cement. The steps toward my two bedroom apartment cause more anguish than relief. My shoes scrape against the concrete of the sidewalk, leaving black scuff marks. All of today, I tried to keep from getting here, from coming home.

"Honey, I'm home," I announce to no one in particular. My keys drop to the floor when I miss the nail in the wall where I keep all of my keys and sunglasses.

I use the heel of each foot to take the shoes off and kick them off to the sides of my recliner. It looks so comfortable. Sorry, old friend. I'm going to your biggest competition: the bed.

My air conditioning turns on instantly when I get to my bedroom, a sure-fire sign that I'm going to be welcomed with open arms into Slumberland.

I take my shirt off over my head despite it having buttons and drop my pants. I hit the bed and bounce, closing my eyes and the first thing I see is Brandon's face, smiling at me.

At first I try to smile, but I blink when I think I feel something touching my toes. I look down, nothing but bed sheets and a comforter, so I close my eyes again, and the darkness of my eyelids has now been splattered with Brandon's bloody face, his eyes missing and a gaping hole in the middle of his nose.

My heart goes into overdrive, and my reaction makes me grab a pillow and hug it tightly. I take calm breaths, breathe in the good. Breath out the bad. Stress out. Calm in. My eyes search the room for something to focus on, a spot on the wall that doesn't somehow remind me of what used to be. My eyes glance at the pile of clothes that I couldn't wash. All of them belonged to Brandon.

My pulse causes my neck to beat in time with my heart.

Pulse pulse. Pulse pulse.

Breathe in. Breathe out. Calm in. Stress out.

My eyes look at the sides of the collar of the top golfer's shirt. He never wanted to golf, but liked the look. My eyes trace the faint orange threads of the jeans he wore, now apparently coming apart, and I blink. We need a new washer, and I needed to get rid of that shit a long time ago.

No rest. There will be no rest here.

Can't sleep, so I get up from the bedroom and follow the walls to the kitchen, where I open the refrigerator and mourn the empty shelves and overpopulated refrigerator door, now overrun with condiments. Why do I need three types of mustard?

When the glare of the fridge light gets to be too much on my eyesight and gives permission for a headache to start kicking around in my cranium, I realize that all is lost and maybe I should do without the snack for now. I could spare a few pounds, after all.

It's when I realize that I need noise that I turn on the television and wait for the people on the news channels to tell me something good. Instead, at this late hour of the night, I'm catching cable network news: people I've never seen before—obviously the

B-listers—telling me that the Middle East is going to Hell in a hand basket, our president apparently hates us, and we are still waiting for equal rights to marry other men. No news there.

This is the point where I'd hand the remote over to Brandon and let him pick something while I rested my head on his shoulder. I try to close my eyes and rest against the side of the armchair recliner, but I can't find a spot that welcomes my head anywhere. I force my eyes to open, to focus on something else, and I find something immediately in the television screen: a light blue face looking back at me. The outlines and shadows of the face turn and interrogate me with pissed-off glances. The hair falls over the eyebrows and the cheeks still have a puffy youthfulness to them. The lips hold tightly against themselves as the head turns left, then right, then stares right at me.

I'm getting way too tired for this. More shadows and more illusions. I'm too damned old for this. The eyes look familiar, faded and hidden behind deep brow ridges. The shadows turn into light blue lines, and for a second I could swear I see the face smile at me, and then turn away.

Brandon.

It was him.

Brandon, I love you.

I want to believe that this is just the maddening rantings of a man who lost his boyfriend. That painful sadness that overcomes the brain and heart when you just don't know where to go or who to turn to.

So, I do what I know I should have done a long time ago and head into the kitchen.

The cupboards' shelves nearly bend under the weight of our—I mean my—glasses and plates and bowls and everything we--I mean I--worked hard at to keep the same. When the time came to move in, we went shopping.

It was my idea, for the record.

Blue violets, intertwined at the stem, trace the edges of our plates and bowls. It was something manly—I'm gay, not a woman—and still soothing during our evening dinners.

Those dinners won't happen anymore.

Each flower-lined bowl and plate comes out of that shelf and onto the counter. Stacked in dangerous heights, the bowls wobble as they are placed on top of plates on top of glasses on top of more bowls.

Say good-bye.

My arm reaches for the window just above the sink, and I open it. I toss a bowl at the window, out into the darkness, but it comes back at me and shatters onto the floor.

"God dammit!" I growl and check my bare feet for splinters or cuts. "Where are you?" I shout at the window. I'm sure my neighbors are loving this. "Where the fuck are you!" My hands grasp for the edges of the window, and there's the reason everything came back to me: I had a screen across the opening.

And though I'm laughing, I'm so pissed off, gnashing my teeth together. With the closest knife I can find—a butterknife—I hack and slash at the black screen. The slashing blade bends the gray metal frame until it falls out into the yard and frayed nylon screen appears to be growing from the serrated edges of the knife.

And the show begins. First a bowl, then pieces of the shattered bowl at my feet. Out of the window, one by one. No thoughts come into my head, nothing leaves my lips. Not a single thought except everything must go. A plate wavers slightly as the wind carries it up and over my windowsill. Next goes a glass, frosted at the bottom to make it look like an ice-cold chilly drink. Brandon's favorite for punch.

Then goes the Sesame Street coffee mug. Don't ask.

The soup bowls.

Then another plate, finishing off our four-piece matching set.

And looking for more to throw, my hand reaches and grabs nothing. I can't let this be, my heart still thumping, and I open up the drawers and dig in. The metal clashes and crunches against each other in large clusters in my hand. Out they go, some hitting the wall and falling back inside the sink. Others are released out into the wild, straight as an arrow into the night sky.

Good bye, Brandon.

Good bye, memories.

Good bye, good bye, good bye.

Nearly every cabinet is open when my lungs gasp for breath, and I can barely move a muscle. Shattered ceramic and paint and metal eating utensils litter my kitchen floor, and for once, I don't care.

The soles of my feet grab hold of splintered ceramic and carry the pieces with me onto the carpet, wiping traces of red blood along my path to the master bathroom. My shoulders feel too heavy to lift, my arms dragging the way a gorilla's arms feel when he walks. Who would have thought purging your kitchen of memories would be such great exercise?

The shower comes on hot right away, the pipes in the walls crying out in pain. I take off my shirt and wonder when the hell I got so fat. Fat and hairy, though I haven't trimmed in a little over a month. My boxers hit the floor around my ankles in a bunch, and it's hard to not feel aroused by the workout, the adrenaline, and the thrill of destroying things.

I grip the sliding glass door, which rolls open with ease. With my eyes closed, stepping into the beats of water blasting against my pudgy body, I think it's just my imagination when a sound of what I think are footsteps touches my ears.

"You're not exactly an easy guy to scare," says a voice that's way too familiar.

"Joey! How the hell did you get in here?" My hands grab for my junk, and though the glass is frosted like most shower glass doors are, I know for a fact that you can see outlines and shades of light and dark.

"I'm looking up, you perv," he says. "No one is interested in your junk."

"Get out," I scream.

"You should really lock your doors," he says. "Any idiot can walk right in."

"Too easy," I say. "Why are you here?"

"We need to go," he says. "Get your towel."

"Get out," I say. "Where are we going?"

"You'll see."

The adrenaline from earlier still hasn't filtered through my system, something I'm sure that Joey wasn't aware of, so his blurry body jumps into the air when I scream out, "Get. The. Fuck. Out!"

The door slides open with a push of my hand, and Joey stands before me. His black hoodie drapes loose over his body, more so than before, and the hood fully covered his head. Just the tip of his pale chin poked through the darkness and reflected some of the fluorescence from the bathroom mirror lights.

When I try to get a better look at his face, my vision blurs.

"Um, towel?" he says. "I thought guys were supposed to get bigger when you get older."

I wrap the closest towel around my waist, tucking in the sides. "Get out."

I throw on pants, shirt, shoes, and gun and follow him out to my car, he leads me the way a woman leads a puppy to the side of the car. And he points at the road from inside, through the windshield. "Drive."

And at this point, my eyes see nothing but red and my heart pumps battery acid through my veins. I just draw my gun and press it against the side of his head. "Not until you tell me where are you taking me?"

Joey's face never turns toward me, just stares straight ahead of us. "Put the gun away, Robbie."

The gun barrel digs further into his hood. "I don't see why I should."

"Because I asked nicely," he said.

"I'm sorry," I say and press the barrel so hard into

the hood that Joey's head bends at the neck at a forty-five degree angle. "That's not good enough reason."

"You're an idiot, Robbie."

"An idiot with a gun," I say.

"And you still don't believe me," he says. His head bends at a forty-seven degree angle, forty-eight, fifty, fifty-five, as my anger takes hold of my better judgment. "Fine," he says. His hands rise up, a surrender, and his right hand reaches slowly to the passenger's side door. "I'll just have to show you."

"Fine. Get out." My left hand grasps the door, and I step out, expecting him to stand out.

Then, even though I didn't realize that the door didn't even open, there is Joey standing in front of the car. The headlights turn on and Joey's black hoodie drapes open, his body disappearing into the shadows of his own jacket.

My mouth opens, but I don't know what to say. The lights of the car flash off and on, and then finally click off. His body floats near me, with only the tips of his shoes scraping against the asphalt road, he stops just a few inches from my face.

"Are you now ready to listen?" he says in a raspy, slow voice.

When I reach out for his face, I grab nothing, his body now six inches further back. "What are you?" I ask. I take a step forward, grabbing for his jacket, and each time nothing remains in my reach. "What?"

"I said are you ready to listen?" he asks.

My feet won't move. As hard as I think I'm pulling on my feet, I can't move, my feet glued to the road. "How are you doing this?"

"I was hoping you'd just listen and do what I say," he says, "but it appears that we're going to have to do this the hard way." The shadows of his chest heave up and down in what is probably a sigh, and he says, "Get back into the car."

"What are you?"

"I told you ghost, but you wouldn't listen," he says. "Can you now get into the car?" Joey's feet drop onto the surface of the street, and he waves a hand at my car door for me to get in. "C'mon."

NINE

He directs me to my department. During the drive, I'm silent. Scared shitless. But once we're at work, Joey leads me back to my desk and stands just a picture of me and Brandon, laying flat on my desk. "We need to talk," he says.

"We couldn't do this in the car?" I say. My hands lay buried deep in my pockets, hugging close to my body.

"Nope," he says. "Sit, he'll be here any minute."

Because I honestly don't see any reason arguing with this kid, I just take a seat and twiddle my thumbs. First twirling forward, then backward. Joey rests his ass on the top of desk, legs dangling and kicking the front of my metal desk.

"What are we waiting for?" I ask.

Joey smiles, pulls his hood even further across the front of his face and smiles showing teeth.

"Robert!" says Chief. "What the hell are you doing here?" Chief Kerry rests his hand on my shoulder, squeezes with his fingers and says, "I was going to call you earlier this morning, but we can talk about this now, if you're up to it."

"I guess this depends on what we're talking about, sir," I say. When I look across my desk to see if this is what Joey was talking about, he's not sitting there.

"Sir?" I ask.

"What is it, Lambert?"

"Did you see…" and I stop my statement before I can finish it. I already seem like a ranting lunatic. "You know what, never mind, I wouldn't want you to spoil it for me."

"See, this is the shit we need to talk about, Robert." Chief grabs my shoulder and pulls me up to stand. "Follow me."

We go to the office of no return, his spacious office where everyone confesses secrets, deals are made, and people are nailed against the wall for things they've done.

"Forensics has been sitting in this for a while because I asked them to, Robert, but your actions lately tell me that you need to have some consequences for your actions." Kerry takes a seat and extends an open hand to the chair across from his desk. I take the hint and plant my ass in the chair.

I think I know where this is going, and images of me running out of the office run through my head. Just how far could I get before he catches me? He's overweight, hasn't been to PT in years.

"We know where the bullets came from," he says.

Awkward silence as he waits for me to show my hand. He wants me to finish the sentence to make this easier for me.

"I'm unsure what you mean," I say. And of course, I'm lying to him. Maybe I can make this extend longer than necessary; turn this into a convoluted mess and blame forensics for messing up. There's gotta be a way out of this.

"Normally, we'd be more than willing to look the other way on something like this. One of the," Kerry takes a pause, looking for the right word, "benefits of my position." He leans his body forward like he's trying to hide his words from someone else in the office. "We have to talk about why you shot your partner." He sits back. "Especially since considering," he pauses again, searching for more words. "You know."

"That I was fucking Brandon?" I say. Fire courses through my veins.

"Is that what this is all about?" I stand, indignant like, try to keep my level of control in this conversation. "You're going to frame me for the death of my partner so you can have my badge?"

"Is that really what you think this is?" Kerry stands up, rests his hands on the desk and looks directly into my eyes, his pupils dilating and digging into my soul. "You really think you're that fucking important to this department? Do you not realize that I've been covering your ass for years? All of those faulty arrests? You've shot more people than you know, and I've had to deal with the brunt of the public's overall negative image of us, all because of you and your faggot boyfriend."

"Are we done, sir?" I say. My hand is already on my gun, ready to hand it over or shoot him, I don't know just yet.

"We're not done yet, and you sit your ass back down." He points at the chair. "Sit the hell down," he says. "Did I say I was going to fire you?"

No. No, he didn't.

I sit down, cross my legs to keep me from stammering my feet on the floor. "What else do you want?"

"You've not been going to your psych evals," he says. "I can't help you if you won't help me in this manner."

"I'm not going to get evaluated. Last time I did that, some asshole tried to say I was gay because I didn't have a strong relationship with my dad."

"I could give a rat's ass what you think, Lambert. I need you to keep up appearances. I need you to be respectful while I try to figure out what the hell to do with your dumb ass."

A knock on the door echoes into the office at 2:34 a.m., and we both look at each other in surprise, Kerry and me. "Are you expecting anyone?" I ask.

"Don't be cute," he says. He comes around his office desk, opens the door and no one is there. "What kind of game is this?" he says. Kerry sticks his head and shoulders outside and looks right, then left. He shuts the door and turns to me. "You heard that, too, right?"

"Yup." After this, I blink, and blink again, and Joey stands behind my boss—or would-be ex-boss— and his hands, though seemingly invisible to everyone else, shoves my boss out into the office area and slams the door tight with just a wave of his hand.

"We need to go," Joey says. His voice dark and raspy. "I don't have time for this."

"And how do you suspect we get out of here?" I

say. "Can you make me invisible, too?"

Joey's head cocks to the side, thinking. "You know, I don't know if I can or not. Never tried."

Waiting for the other shoe to drop, I say, "So?"

"Oh, we're not doing this just yet."

Kerry's hands slam into the door. "Who the hell are you talking to?" he says. "Open this door, or it'll be your ass!" he shouts. Kerry's meaty hands slam into the doors again and again and again. "Open this damned door!"

The door handle rattles.

"Is he always this angry?" Joey asks.

"Oh ya. Comes with the job."

"That explains the heart attack, I guess," Joey says, but then looks over at me.

"What heart attack?" I ask.

"This one," he says, and Joey snaps his fingers. The door opens just long enough for me to take a step back and Kerry's body slumps to the floor. His right hand grabs the left side of his chest, and he looks at me.

Someone is coming in to the office from the sound of the office door opening.

"Please," Kerry says. "Please." His right hand clutches his chest so hard his knuckles turn white, veins popping out. "Call. Nine. One. One."

"We don't have time for this," says Joey. "No one

can help him anyway."

I grab the office phone anyway, dial 9-1-1 and wait for the operator to answer.

"9 1 1, what is your emergency?"

"Come on," says Joey. "We can't stay here." His head turns to the front of the office, where a woman—an officer I don't recognize right now, and don't have the time to look through my rusty memory—comes into the office.

She takes a pause, puts her hand to her mouth and says, "What the? Chief?" The mystery officer's first reaction is to run toward us.

Joey looks at me, "See? Do you want to be accused of murder for a second time tonight?"

Joey brings up an excellent point, and while I'm wondering just how he knew about the heart attack.

Joey disappears, and then reappears just a few feet in front of us, and like a line of bread crumbs, I follow his disappear and reappearing act around the office and furniture.

"Who are you?" says the mystery police officer. In my civilian clothing, I don't look like a cop, and therefore more suspicious.

God dammit.

"Stop!" she says. The officer draws her gun on me, aiming and threatening to fire, but in the office, that would be one of the stupidest things she could do. One shot and the entire office building would be out of here, causing a panic. If people panic, help can't get into the building to help Kerry.

I don't know if she's smart enough to figure all of this out, so I help to call her bluff.

The path the Joey leads me through takes me around the southern wall of the office, nearest the windows and the bathroom. My back scratches on a small red box hanging on the wall. A fire alarm.

Perfect.

I pull the alarm, waiting for more chaos, and the officer puts her gun back into her holster and kneels back down to Kerry's body. I can't hear what's going on, but the deafening sound of the high-pitched electronic screams make it damn near impossible to hear what's going on.

I search for my next path through the office, and Joey stands near the stairwell door of our two-floor department building. The fire alarm drowns out his words, and I could never read lips.

"What?" I shout out to him. The look on his eyes tells me to freeze what I'm doing. The doors open. Men and women wearing our midnight blue uniforms storm into the office and rush right past me. My body—maybe because I'm pressed up against the wall, maybe because of the noise and the confusion of the fire alarm—is just not visible to them right now. Either way, I take a deep breath and hold it, like those extra one or two inches from my stomach will really keep me from being seen.

Three more people come in, bursting through the doors and through Joey's immaterial form. I am unsure I will ever get used to seeing that.

The faint sounds of "Over here!" sound through the office. The boys in blue, they rush over to where the mystery co-worker waves her arms, flagging down the help in a last ditch effort to save my boss's life.

I feel a tug on the sleeve of my shirt, and Joey's body is suddenly next to mine, smelling like nothing at all despite the tension and rush of adrenaline we've both got to be feeling. "Come," he says.

His body pulls me further. The funny thing is, my body feels like it's running, too, running despite the fact that I don't know that my legs are moving. I look down and yes, I'm running, but detached from the rest of my body. Whatever I'm doing, it's not because I'm telling it to.

"Where are we going to?" I ask while we're midway down the steps.

"No questions," he says. "Must run."

"Will Kerry be okay?" I ask.

Joey's head turns toward me while we're flying down the stairs, through the downstairs office and out into the foyer, into the alleyway just across the street. "No," he says. "I'll have to come back for him later."

"Wait, what?" I ask.

"That was pretty cool," he says.

"We just killed my boss, pulled a fire alarm, and I had a gun pulled on me." My chest feels empty, and as many times as I try to take a breath, I can't seem to get enough air into my system. I say, "What part of that was cool?"

"Oh that? Pfft," he says. He waves his arm, dismissing it. "I wasn't talking about that. Remember that question you asked about making you invisible, too?"

I nod.

"I totally can."

TEN

Joey's next lofty idea brings us back to the ice cream store at the end of Main Street. We go by car, taking every backstreet I can remember and driving as quickly as possible. My goal? Not to get caught by someone who might be on duty at this hour.

Thanks to Joey's shenanigans, I'm probably going to have uniformed officers after me to answer questions for something I didn't do.

At least, I don't think I did anything.

The street lights buzz above us as we cross over the street and enter into the front doorway of the closed-down ice cream store.

"Why are we here?" I ask.

"Shh," he says. He brings his fingers up to his lips, presses them against his face and before my eyes, the outlines of Joey begin to fade until there is nothing left in front of me.

My expression is I don't know what. What do you say when you see someone just reappear and disappear in your very eyes?

Joey's form takes shape inside the ice cream parlor. His shadow glides over the construction site inside, the hammers and wooden sawhorses seem to fade as he walks through them, only to reappear after he's done walking to the front of the store and politely flicks the switch to let me in.

"How can you do that?"

"A gift," he says. "Or a curse. Depends on how you look at it, really." Joey leads me to the back of the store and in the left of the backroom is an office, door closed tightly with the yellow Do Not Enter strips across it. "Here," he says.

With those words, Joey puts his hand through the door and opens it, pulling his hand out, his fleshy hand disappearing back into his jacket sleeve.

"Neat trick," I say.

When the door swings open, what's left is a darkened stain on the wall, a splatter of blood—my guess—and more blackened stains on the wooden shelf-desk thing attached to the wall.

"Why are we here?" I ask.

"This," says Joey, slowly and sad. "This was me." He raises his arm and the flowing of his black jacket seems to wave in imaginary, nonexistent wind.

"This is your blood?" I ask.

His hood nods up and down. I peek closer, squinting my eyes, but Joey's facial features suddenly disappear while I'm peeking. That feeling you get when something is just outside of your vision? How it disappears when you look at it head on? That's what happens when I try to get a fix on Joey's face when he's in one of these moods.

"Why bring me here?" I ask. "Why do I need to see this?"

"This store was my dad's. I worked the morning shifts in the summer, when school was out."

As he told the story, the image if this boy, sunshine blond hair and bright sky-blue eyes, perky in the morning churning ice cream or whatever they did to get themselves ready for the morning.

"I was getting something ready when a little teenager came to the front door." Joey's body turns, smooth as silk, toward the office door. "It was too early to open still, so I decided to let them know." Like an extension of his face, the hood widens as if his head is smiling inside. "The boy didn't take no for an answer. He kept knocking and knocking and knocking."

This was a story that was beginning to sound familiar, but I wasn't quite sure where I had heard it from. It was thought to be an urban legend, one of the fifty million that seem to pervade Saraday lore. But this time--this time it seemed to be more believable. My eyes widened as he told this story, careful not to interrupt his heart-to-heart moment.

"I ignored him as much as I could. I could swear I was hearing my dad's voice in my head as the boy kept knocking and knocking, then slamming and slamming on the front door." The dark hood seems to pause to swallow, then continues. "I couldn't take it anymore, I wasn't even sure that this guy was even hearing me when I came out of the office, the boy had a rock in his hand. He looked happy, but twisted. He was knocking the rock on the glass, this chang-chang against the glass. I went to the window and tried to shush him away. I remember telling him 'We don't open for another hour. Sorry.'"

Another pause and the hood says, "That's when he decided that he was going to push the window open. He saw me, and must have got scared and figured that I saw him, so he got aggressive. He hit the window, then tried to push it open, like he was somehow going to break through the glass. When he finally got a dent chipped into the glass, I got scared and opened the door. Mistake number one."

Joey turns to face the blood and points over at the makeshift desk. "This is where he took me after he got in. The first thing he did was hit me across the face with the rock, then he dragged me back to the office. He wanted all of the money, so I gave him everything we had. As he took the money and tried to stuff it into his pockets, he began to pivot like he was going to turn around, so I tried to stab him with a pen." There's a pause, and his hood looks to the ground. "He was faster than I was, I guess, and saw me coming. He wrestled the pen out of my hand and managed to stab me in the neck three times before leaving me with the pen still in my neck as he left the store."

"You were that kid," I say. "I thought it was just another urban legend.'

"You and a lot of other people. My dad tried to keep the store open when after I died. He was so ashamed of everything that had happened, he tried to clean all of this up, but was couldn't deal with the fact that he was alive, and I was dead. Instead, he just simply locked this door and moved the office to the side of the store. He wanted to prove to the town that he wasn't shattered by the death of his son. Maybe try to prove to them that they didn't win, so he went to work earlier and earlier every day. Left later and later, until finally, it nearly cost him my mother."

"I'm sorry to hear that."

"I've been stuck here since, trying to—" he pauses, then shakes his head. "We'll cross that bridge later," he says.

"Why bring me here?" I ask. "This has nothing to do with me."

"But you were trying to bring me home," he says. Joey brings his hand across the bloody stains. His fingers trace the outlines of the splatter on the wall, the puddle on the top of the shelf. "Now you can see why you could never win. You couldn't take me home. I have no home."

"Then why me?" I ask. "Why show up for me?"

"Have you ever heard of the phrase quid pro quo?" he asks. His head nods up and down, sizing up my reaction to his story. "I share this, so you can share later."

"And what, exactly, am I supposed to share?"

"Share your pain, your hurt. Deal with your issues, Robert. Nothing can get better until it finally gets acknowledged. My father had to give up the entire store and move on. But, funny thing is, he wasn't able to step into this very office because he couldn't acknowledge my death and his pain. The keeping it all in, it was his way of dealing with things, but it doesn't work exceptionally well when it's in your face day in and day out."

"Fine, I'm damaged. Is that what you wanted to hear?"

"I don't believe you, Robert."

"You don't believe that I'm damaged?" This is getting ridiculous, so I take a step out of the office, out of the direction of his hood, whichever way his mysteriously hidden eyes are facing. Me or the wall, I can't tell.

"I don't believe that you're ready to acknowledge it," he says.

"And so you're here to save me?" I say. "That's rich."

"Sometimes it's never the ones you expect, Robert. I would have thought your line of work would have taught you that much." Joey's legs don't appear to move, but his body floats out of the back office and the door closes behind him. As he brushes past me, I feel a sensation of deep cold, a chill in my bones so deep that I can't even bring myself to shiver. "You're a lost cause, Robert."

"Then leave me alone then." I walk to the front of

the store, secretly racing against his legless movements, wondering just how fast can I get to the car before he can follow me. "Now that you're finally—" I pause and open my arms to embrace the entire insides of the store, "home or whatever, then you don't need me."

"That was never the question," he says. "You need me."

ELEVEN

My engine stalls before it finally turns over, and though I'm not willing to admit it evenly, I know it was Joey trying to keep me there. "It's not going to work!" I shout out into the humid early morning air. "You can try all you want," I scream.

And the truth is, panic sets in. I don't need this shit any more than he needs to be rehashing his own soul, his own death. He doesn't need to be the person to tell me how to live by showing me how he died.

I don't need to hear any of this. I don't need it, I don't want it.

"You hear that!" I scream out into the air, for good

measure. "I don't need you!"

A voice from the inside of my car, coming from the backseat, says, "Yes, you do, and the sooner you admit it, the better for you."

"For me?" I say with a chuckle. "For me?"

I slam on the gas and tires squeal out into the dawn. If the boys in blue weren't looking for me before, they sure as hell are now. "You can't do anything to me."

I take a quick glance into the rearview mirror and spot Joey sitting in middle of the seat, staring back at me, his chin lit up in the streetlights coming in through the windows. "You're such an idiot. It's amazing that you haven't died yet."

"Yet?" I say.

"Yet," he says and crosses his arms. "And you might want to watch out in front of you. There's a metal barrier."

Sure as shit, when I look up, I spot the metal barrier, an old separation to keep the old drivers from going into the flooded ditches that carry over into the Columbia River some thirty miles up east. "Don't tell me how to drive!" I take a quick jerk of the wheel to the right, turning up Diamond Street, and press the gas. I'm leaning into the turn, so I don't notice the centripetal motion as much, but when I glance back to see how my backseat driver is doing, he sits calm and still. "Stupid, stupid, ghost."

"You're not really going to get anywhere behaving like a child, Robbie."

"I'm not behaving like a child! I just want to be left alone!" I lean my body and jerk the wheel a hard left, then a hard right.

"You've drawn attention to yourself," he says.

As I glance up into the rearview to shoot Joey a glance, lights flash behind me—red and blue—and my instinct takes over, pressing the gas as hard as I can and gunning it down the street.

"This is so infantile," he says. "I tried to help you, and you freak out like a little baby, and this is what you get: A free ticket to jail. Do not pass go, do not collect two hundred dollars." He crosses his hands as he says this, looks into the mirror, and I can see his hooded head turn right, then left, scolding me with a "what the hell" kind of look.

"At least you know you can get out easy," I say. My knowledge of the area isn't that extensive, and as I turn from left to right down the residential streets, it becomes harder and harder for me to figure out where I'm going, or even where I've been. If I were betting man, I'd wager I've been driving in circles for a few seconds now. "Can you at least tell me where I should go?" I ask.

In the mirror, Joey shakes his head.

"Fine then," I say. What appears to be a cul-de-sac in front of me comes quickly, and I realize that if I'm going to lose this asshole, I need to act fast, act on instinct and see where it takes me.

"You don't really want to do that," says Joey.

The police car behind me flashes his brights to get my attention, then announces through his speakers, "You have nowhere to go." There's a pause as I weigh my options. "This is a courtesy, Robert. Stop and we'll work with you."

Bullshit, and we both know it. If they think I killed the chief, then I'm fucked ten times over.

My stomach doesn't know what to do, but the butterflies tell me that I'm probably not making the best decision right now. "Hold on," I say. Then peering up into the mirror again to watch Joey, I say, "Never mind, I forgot who I'm talking to."

I take a hard left with the wheel, and it takes me into another street, something with a "w" at the end of the name, but I missed it as I turned to fast. Though I didn't know where I was heading in the first place, I don't know where I am now, and that makes my heart jump in my chest like a frightened rabbit. "I'm so sorry," I say up into the ceiling of my car. If he is there, if he's watching me and sent this jackass to do something to me, I guess I should get on the Big Guy's side now.

"Are you ready yet?" Joey says.

"Ready?" I ask and look up into the mirror. There is no warning from Joey or the cop behind me when the car jumps the curb. My chin hits my chest and bounces upward, looking at the ceiling, then right in front of me. The front of my car destroys housing brick. Pieces of red brick and dust debris fly in my direction. I take my hands off the wheel and cover my eyes. The car comes to a sudden stop, my seatbelt locks and my neck jerks forward, carrying my head with it. My hands slam against the front windshield and burn from the impact.

The last thing I remember is seeing the red and blues flashing one after another on the dashboard of my car and a final tap on my window, with the words, "Robert?" coming from the mouth of my arresting officer.

TWELVE

My head hurts like it just gave birth, and once I get past the pain of the lights searing into my eyes, I come to the conclusion that I'm in a hospital bed, cuffed and alone. Worse yet, my balls itch, and there's nothing I can do about it.

"Hello?" I announce into the empty room, but no one answers back. "Where am I?" I scream into the emptiness that is my mostly blank hospital room, with an empty bed next to me—mint green sheets and a pillow that's bleached white. "Hello?" I ask. "Anyone?"

"No one will hear you," announces Joey's voice, but there's something hollow about it.

"Joey?" My teeth grind together. "I swear to God, if you're here, in this room, I'll fucking kill you. I'll kill you again and again and again."

"Ghost? Remember that detail?" he says. Nobody steps out of the room's vast emptiness. When you're alone with your own thoughts, and the voices of dead friends, the room you're in seems so much bigger. Any given side of the room feels like it would take an eternity to reach.

Especially if you're in handcuffs.

"Get me out of here," I say. "Please, I swear that I won't hurt you."

"You can't hurt me, moron."

I close my eyes, tell myself that it's okay for him to call me moron. Anything to get this little son of a you-know-what to get me out of the cuffs and out of this bed. "Why am I here?"

"Because you need to learn," he says.

I roll my eyes.

"I can see that, you know," says Joey's hollowed voice. The tones of his syllables bounce around in the room, off walls or the inside of my head, I can't tell. But with each bounce, it gets louder, more stern, like a father scolding a son. "And if that's the attitude you're going to have, we've already made this a pointless visit."

"Visit?" I say. Visit means I get to leave, means I

don't have to stay in these cuffs, means I can scratch my balls.

"Only if you play nicely," he says. "Does Room 14 mean anything to you?"

My heart sinks, bobbing in my stomach.

"I'll take that frown as a yes," he says. "Take a look."

I don't know why I stop breathing, why I can't seem to figure out whether I'm supposed to breathe in or breathe out. I don't know why my brain suddenly can't figure out what I'm doing and why I'm even here.

All I know is, I need to leave. I need to get out. I jingle the handcuffs against the metal railing, shouting, "Let me out!" at the top of my lungs, but no one comes in—and believe you me, I watch the door closely.

My face feels hot and itchy from the inside. An allergic reaction? To what?

"Help!" I scream louder, my neck strains, muscles tense up and stretch like twine, little strands uncurling. My eyes close, and I focus on my breathing. Think about the sunlight, think about a calm, relaxing space.

"This is where he died, you know, in your own very little bed."

And you know what? Screw the sunlight. Screw the calm. Screw the relaxing space. Screw it all. My heart pumps louder, audible in my chest, driving me like a bass drum hooked to a car battery. Revving the engine, my heart beats faster and faster. It beats the beads of sweat off of my brow, on my neck, on my chest under this white undershirt. Suddenly, it feels scorching hot and freezing cold at the same time.

A panic attack.

"I," I wheeze. "Can't."

"Yes, you can," he says.

I try to close my eyes, to filter out the room, but when I do, Brandon's auburn hair—that same hair that I rubbed my hands through over and again in nightly passions—drips with sweat on the flat and firm hospital pillow. His eyes widen, the green almost seems to flare into the fluorescent lights above. His mouth cries out as he looks at me with hate, with anger.

When I open my eyes, the images of his death fills the rest of the room, like holograms in a virtual reality. I swear I can see the crash carts, the nurses and doctors. Though no one else is in the room, I know there are echoes of crying, yelling orders, commands to get out of the room, to save my dying boyfriend. To do everything you can save him.

Warm tears fill the lower gaps of my eyelids, then flood out down my cheekbones and soaking the pillow and bed underneath me. My hands pull tighter against the cuffs. I know they are cutting into my wrists, but the adrenaline and fear and panic and prevents me from knowing the difference between pain and freedom.

"Joey!" I scream. "Get me out of here!" Tears well up so that I can barely see the colors of the walls and outlines of the rest of the furniture. "Please, just get me out of here," I say. My chest heaves between syllables. My words feel heavy when I cry for a release from everything. "Don't just leave me here."

When I close my eyes, Brandon's face reveals a hatred for me. When I open them, I relive the moment as echoes of reality.

Damned if I do, damned if I don't.

"Joey!"

Silence except for the jingling of my handcuffs and my cries out into the emptiness.

The door cracks open, and beams of light shed light on the foot of my bed. Beams of freedom, I hope. "Shut up in there!" says a man's head. Security guard judging by the colors of his uniform. "You're going to wake the dead," he says with a smile.

"That guy's funny," says Joey.

"Get me out, please!" I say.

The guard looks at me and shakes his head. "Well, since you asked nicely," he says and then laughs to himself. My pain and suffering becomes a joke to this two-bit asshole. At least they could get real cops helping me.

"If they got real cops helping you," says Joey's voice, "then they'd run the risk of having them either hurt you on the spot for killing the captain, or of having you get yourself out of here by sweet-talking the help."

Dammit.

Breathe slowly, Robert. Breathe slowly in, breathe out.

"Get me out of here, please," I say.

The guard closes the door with an echo.

"You leave when I'm done," Joey says.

"I'm sorry, okay," I announce. "I'm sorry for everything."

"You're getting warmer, Robbie," says Joey.

"What do you want from me? What do you want?" More tears stream down my face. My wrists burn from cutting them on the cuffs. My whole body aches and feels relaxed at the same time. Tiring myself out with each panic attack. "Just make it stop," I say. "Please."

The door cracks open again, and a tall man walks into the room with confidence, an arrogant confidence that tells me he's either a political figure or Internal Affairs.

"Scott Wilkes," says the man. "Pleased to meet you, Robert." Scott stops only a few feet away from me, looks me up and down, analyzes the cuffs and then winces as his eyes meet the cuts on my cuffs. "That was unnecessary, you know." Scott Wilkes has to be about six-feet-three, probably works out whenever he feels like it and eats like a Californian, vegetables and avocados and shit. He runs his hand through his hair—parted on the left side—using his left hand—no ring on any finger on both hands. Either married to his job or gay. The hand through your hair bit is supposed to make me think that he's not enjoying this, that he's just as stressed about this as I am. It's bullshit, but I go with it anyway.

Wilkes unbuttons his suit jacket with his right hand—still no ring confirmed—in order to make it look like he's ready to calm down a little bit, get on my level.

"We can do this a couple of ways," he says. "We can either help you get out of here, and you cooperate with us with the truth, or we can go ahead and keep you locked up and send your stupid ass to prison as soon as you heal up from your nasty head wound."

"Fuck off," I say.

"That was pretty much the reaction I was hoping for," he says.

"When you're ready to cooperate with us, and tell us what really happened that night of your partner's shooting, just let me know, will you?" The door clicks behind him when he leaves the room.

"Check and check," says Joey's voice.

"What the hell is that for?" I ask.

"You're just getting started, big boy," he says.

"Don't call me big boy," I say. "I swear, I don't know what he's talking about. I don't know what he wants me to tell him."

"You're lying, Robbie." Joey steps out from behind a veil of thin air, his black coat still draped over him. With his hood still extended over his head, locks of dirty blond hair escape from around his forehead. "How do you expect me to trust you if you keep lying to me?"

"Trust me?" I ask. "Trust? Me?" My face feels bright red, boiling blood under my skin, the way I get when I'm about to blow a gasket. "You mean to tell me, after all that I've tried to do for you, or alive you, or whatever the hell you are, and you don't trust me?"

"Relax, Robbie. I was only kidding. You're way too old for this kind of thing. You need to watch that old ticker. Especially since you refused to watch the ol' cholesterol."

"Fuck you," I say and turn my head away from him. "Just leave me alone."

"You'll go back to the station where they'll leave you in holding until they can get a confession out of you," says Joey. And though his ghostly presence sends a slight tingle down my spine, I feel the weight of his corporeal form rest on the foot of the bed. "And let's face it, this is a small town in Podunk, South Carolina. They can pretty much do whatever they want to your ignorant ass."

"Why do you tell me these things?" I say. "What am I supposed to do?"

"I need to get you ready," he says. Then a pause and his head turns away from me, looks to the door. "Forget you heard that last part."

"Heard what?"

"Good for you, Robbie. That's what I'm talking about," he says. His hand pats me on the leg through the mint green blanket that covers me, and he stands up. "Let me see what I can do."

"You put me in this mess," I say. "Now you get me out of it."

Joey points to his chest. "Remember the old ticker." He puts his hand to his chin, thinking. "Just give me a second."

And though Joey doesn't need to, he opens the door and taps my giant would-be guard on the shoulder. The man's head slumps over as if he's listening, and then there's a dull thump of something heavy hitting the floor.

Joey walks in, his hands slapping each other like a job well done, and he walks over to me. "That should get someone's attention," he says.

"Did you kill him?" I ask.

"Kill?" he says. He shrugs and pretends that he's insulted. "Heavens no. I just gave him a near-life experience."

"Isn't that a near—" I begin to say when a female orderly walks past the door and stops, then stares at me.

"Oh my god, is this man okay?" she says.

I shrug because honestly, I have no idea.

"Let me call for help," she says. She comes into the room, picks up the phone and dials some numbers into the phone. "I need someone down the emergency wing, by Room 14. One of the security—" she takes a glance outside at him. "I think he passed out or something." Another pause. "Yes, it looks like he's breathing. Just come down here." She hangs up the phone and steps outside. "Don't you worry," she says to me, like I give a rat's ass about this guy. "Help is coming."

"For me or for him?" I ask.

The orderly looks puzzled and scrunches her eyebrows.

"Never mind," I say. "And by the way, he was my guard, not my friend."

She still looks puzzled, so I leave her be. No use trying to stress herself out by explaining it further.

As more orderlies and doctors appear by my door, I notice that Joey stands at the entryway, watching the goings on and commenting on the way that the people decide to haphazardly lift the guard's body and take him to a nearby resting spot.

"Are you sure you didn't kill him?" I ask.

"Pretty sure, ya," he says.

A pair of dress shoes clicks on the tile floor, and a voice gets louder as the source comes closer down the hallway. "We're going to need to get him out of here," a man's voice says. "If he's good to go, I want him moved to the station where he can stay in holding all night, as far as I'm concerned." The shoes stop and squeak as he turns around, and someone who belongs to that voice appears around the opened doorway. "What the hell happened to Jameson?" he says.

I recognize that voice and suit.

Wilkes appears back into the room. "Get up, we're leaving," he says.

I raise my hands up as far as the limited chains on the cuffs will allow.

"Oh, right," he says, scratching his head. "Forgot about that." He pops his head out into the hallways, shouting at everyone passing by. "Can we get some keys for some cuffs in here?" he asks. "Thanks."

"We're going back to holding," he says.

"I heard," I say. Less than thrilled, but at least I get out of here. The cuffs were making me claustrophobic.

"Ya, my wife always said I was always too loud," he says. He sticks his head out into the doorway again, impatient. "You have some answers to a few questions we need."

A man—some lowly officer who was probably standing at the front of the hospital—comes into the room and uncuffs my hands long enough to get them free, then announces to me, "Hands in front where I can see you," he says.

"I'm not going anywhere, Genius," I say. I nod over toward my feet, which are still cuffed to the far end of the bed.

Genius smiles at me and says, "Right." Then, with a puppy dog look that makes me think he's lucky I'm gay, he says for me to keep my hands in front of me so he can put the cuffs back on. I comply and rest my newly re-cuffed wrists on my lap.

"Actually," Wilkes says as the man releases my feet and stands guard back by the door, "we already have all the evidence we need. But we're treating you like a special case since you're one of us." He pauses and continues, "And you killed one of us."

"I didn't kill anyone," he says.

"Ya," he says. He takes a casual step to his left and looks at me through the corner of his left eye. "I don't know about that. You see, we have evidence to the contrary."

"You don't have dick," I say.

"You just can't wait to be in lockup for as long the judge will allow, don't you?" says Wilkes. He smiles to reveal long teeth, small gums, and his face gives an angular impression in this light and with that smile. "You just can't wait to have the whole damn library thrown at you."

"I know what I know," I say. "And you don't have dick."

"You try to pretend like we can't nail you, asshole," he says and takes a step back, waving at Genius. "Take him out of here," he says to Genius, then to me he says, "But we can. We can nail you real hard."

THIRTEEN

We arrive back at the station with a lukewarm welcome and bunch of dirty looks since everyone seems to think that I'm now a cop killer.

"You're looking like you could use a friend," says Hernandez through the glass. In a town like this, we have a temporary holding that is just off the side of the building. The closest county prison is a few dozen miles up the road from here, north of Columbia. Because of that, and no county official wants to head out here on a regular basis to keep track of Saraday, we here at the police department get away with almost anything it wants. Nothing dirty, but let's just say that we can be very convincing to keep creeps out of our town. But only when we need to be.

The sheriff's department doesn't even want to cooperate with us most of the time, just handing over cases if they are even remotely within our jurisdiction. It's these facts that run through my head because I know that we have a reputation for putting people away— or making them go missing. I'm not so afraid of the former, terrified of the latter, and it's those thoughts that make me want to piss myself as I sit and stare at the layers of make up on Hernandez's face.

"I guess you could say that," I say. Since I arrive here, there has been a sudden lack of Joey anywhere, no sign or sound of him. "How are things?"

"They really hate you right now," she says and nods to the front of the building. "Everyone up there. They think you killed the captain."

"I didn't kill anyone," I say. "He had a heart attack, but in this town, they'd rather blame someone than accept it. Easier to just frame the fag."

Hernandez looks to the left and to the right to make sure we're okay. "Why were you there so late?" she asks.

"I don't even know anymore," I say. My last memories of that night before the chaos have me seated in Kerry's room, being threatened, and then him keeling over. I don't remember where Joey was or why he had me take him there. I shrug back at Hernandez. "I don't know what to tell you," I say.

"Then you better think of something fast," she says. "That doesn't exactly help your story."

"I have no motive to kill the captain! What possible reason could I have?"

"Rumor has it he had something on you," she says.

"And if that were true—" it is, but she doesn't need to know this right now—"then why would I still want to kill him? An investigation is just going to bring Internal Affair's eyes even closer to my files. Think about how stupid that is."

"If IA wants someone bad enough," she says. Hernandez doesn't have to finish that sentence because we both know how it ends.

"Then I do what I have to do," I say.

"Which is?" she says. Her palms lay flat against the glass, like I'm going to do some Disney movie emotional moment with her.

"Wait for a friend," I say.

Hernandez takes a step back, crosses her arms and then looks down at me. "I hope you know what you're doing," she says and storms off into the front office.

I want to tell her, "I do," but that would be a lie. Right now my fate seems to be a plaything of a moody seventeen-year-old ghost with a power trip. Ya, this is going to go over well.

I count only an hour, maybe an hour and a half, since I've been sitting in here all by my lonesome, and no sign of the people who locked me up, either. If they're trying to get enough information, then they aren't doing an impressive job of it.

"Joey?" I ask, once again as seems custom, into the cell. Nothing but my own echo comes back to me. I wonder if I'm alone enough to finally piss.

One of the officers walks in with more cuffs as I'm just about ready to fix my pants to piss and walks slow and steady to me. I don't even bother trying to piss now, just follow orders, and maybe they'll leave me alone long enough to figure out just how the hell I'm going to get out of here.

"What's this?" I ask.

"Put these on," says the officer. He slides the cuffs through the slot where the food trays are usually slid in. "You have an interview."

I chuckle to myself. "Interview, huh?"

I slide the cold metal cuffs over my wrists and tighten them, but the officer refuses to budge until I press tight on the bracelet to make sure I'm touching at least two parts of the metal bracelet at all times, not hanging loose off of just one.

"Where to?" I say.

"Follow," he says and unlocks the door. His hand grabs my elbow, and he leads me into the office and down a corridor where we usually keep interrogation suspects. As I traverse from one side of the building to the other, I look out for signs of a black hood, pale white skin, or dirty blond hair. Maybe Joey will make a surprise appearance and spring me while I'm out.

The closer I get to the corridor, however, the more I lose faith in this idea and just reserve my emotions for the outbursts I'll inevitably have when this bullshit continues in the interrogation room.

The officer sits me down in a metal padded chair and affixes the handcuffs to a small stainless steel bar embedded into the interrogation table. "Wait here," he says.

Like I have a choice. I keep my mouth shut and realize suddenly that I have no idea how most suspects actually do this. I mean, it looks easy to sit here and be cool and calm and collected when you're supposed to be the good cop or the bad cop—depending who gets what straw—but it's markedly harder to be that when you're actually cuffed to a table and waiting to see what kinds of questions he's going to ask me.

The door opens, and my main man Wilkes holds a Styrofoam cup of coffee. The steam trails from the door to his current position sitting directly across from me. "So, where were we?" he asks.

"Just how many different conversations are you in at any given time?" I ask.

"You're in luck," he says. Giving any credence to my smartassery would require that he relinquish some of the power to me, something those IA guys just hate to do. "Kerry's death was a heart attack."

"See?" I said. "Told you." I sit back in the chair as far as I can until I realize that my shoulders remain pulled forward by the cuffs that refuse to give any freedom. "Can I go now?"

"Not just yet," says Wilkes. He takes a sip of his coffee to build drama and emotion into his interrogation. He's enjoying this like only a small town officer would. "We need to know why you were there that night. You were off duty—from our understanding almost under suspension—and, yet you still show up at the office and run out when your captain has a heart attack." Wilkes looks at me, licks his lips. "The way I see it, you left because you're hiding something," he says. "Innocent people don't run when there's trouble."

"I was on my way out, couldn't hear anything when the alarms went off," I say. "By the way, shouldn't I be speaking with a lawyer right now?"

"Ya, ya, ya," he says, dismissing me. "We'll get

right on that." Wilkes nods to the giant two-way mirror and then looks at me, nods. "Speaking of that alarm, it's illegal to pull fire alarms as pranks."

"I didn't pull it," I say. Joey, my spirit guide, did, but he wouldn't understand that. "No prints. Check yourself." Nice try, jackass.

"We'll do that," he says. His voice trails again, lost in thought and then he looks at me again. "I think you were there trying to find out what Kerry had on you," he says. He leans in toward the table, like it's just between us—which it's not because he's already established that someone is behind the mirror—and says, "We have the tests."

"You have nothing," I say. "I didn't do anything to him, so unless you're pressing charges, you have to let me free."

"Technically, we still have a few more hours before we legally have to let you go." He looks at the clock on his watch, then shakes his hand to check that it's still ticking. "About three hours and fifty-three minutes to be exact."

Touché, ass wipe.

"I think I need a lawyer," I say. "I'm supposed to have a lawyer present, right?"

Wilkes smiles to hide his contempt for me, then looks at the window and waves at the door. "Fine, have it your way, Lambert, but I wouldn't leave town if I were you." Wilkes stands up and moseys on over to the door. "We'll send someone out to let you free in about," he stops and checks his watch. "Oh, in about three hours and fifty minutes," he says and smiles.

His feet drag on the tiled floor as he leaves me in the interrogation room with just my thoughts. When the door closes, I half expect someone to come popping right in to set me free, but true to his word, I wait and wait for someone to show up. And the door doesn't move. Officers and perps walk past the small vertical window on the door—it's a busy day today—but no one stops to see how I'm doing or what I'm doing. He told everyone that I'm in there, and now he's just going to let me sit and stew in my own frustration and humiliation.

Bastard.

"You can come in whenever you want now," I say and from afar, a hand comes through the door.

"How did you see me?" he says.

"I didn't," I say, then sigh. "You're a little predictable. Spend some time with someone, and you get to know them."

"Aww, you're getting all mushy on me, Detective Robbie." The rest of his body becomes visible as he pulls himself into the room. His first reaction is to look around, and he pouts at the sight of my hands handcuffed to the desk.

"I never said I like this time together," I say.

He looks back at me, smiles. "Now that's the Robbie I know and love." His head analyzes the room, the different dimensions and where each window possibly goes to. "You know, these rooms look a lot larger on television."

"Television?" I say. "If you're getting all of your information from TV, then you've in for a little bit of a surprise."

"I was wondering why this adventure lasted for more than fifty-three minutes," he says with a smile. "In all seriousness, though, how are we going to get you out?" Joey sits down on the chair, rests his elbows on the table and rests his head on his hands. "Hrm?"

"Hell if I know," I say. "Do your magic hocus-pocus stuff."

"Doesn't work like that," he says. He stands up, then walks through the table. With powers like this, I wonder why he isn't just helping me get out and move beyond all of this bullshit. I wonder why he's even bothering with me, for that matter. Clearly he can cause heart attacks. I don't know why he's leaving me alone.

"Am I some cat toy to you?"

His head turns toward me, then the door, then back to me. "I don't quite follow," he says.

"What's with all of this," I say. My hands pull on the cuffs to emphasize my point. "I mean, just kill me already and be done with it."

"Is that what you think I'm here to do?" he says. "Seriously?" His chest heaves up, then holds in his breath, and lets go in a slow, steady sigh. "Robbie, I rather like you." His hands touch his chest. "We bonded." He stands before me and keeps his head facing the window. "But I can't just snap my fingers and let you go. It doesn't work like that." Joey bends over at the waist, looks directly into my eyes. My back shivers, his sky-blue eyes pierce my gaze, looking through me—no, into me—and he smiles. "This is our little secret."

Psycho. This kid is a psycho. A dead, powerful, apparition-like psycho.

"Haven't I suffered enough?" I ask.

He looks at me, smiles at me. "You're going to have to wait a minute," he says.

The door opens suddenly, and Joey takes a step back, probably forgetting that he can't be seen by anyone unless he wants to be. A rather well-built—muscular, not busty—female officer comes into the room holding an old man in her grip. "I'm sorry," she says. "I didn't know this room was taken."

The man in her grip, I recognize the face the instant he peeps into the room, his eyes wandering to get a close look at everything inside.

"Hey," I say. "I know you."

The woman looks at me and looks disappointed. "Yes, you know me, Robert. I work here."

The man in her grip, he looks at the both of us and doesn't look entertained. Pissed off, more like it.

"Not you, ma'am," I say. Words like ma'am get on women's nerves, especially cop women. "That guy," I point with my chin. "That guy right there!"

Joey smiles at me and points. "Yup, you know that guy," he says. "But from where?"

"Again? With this?" I say.

"We just walked in here," says the female officer. She doesn't react to Joey's voice, so he's incognito right now, which means I'm the only one with the pleasure— if you can call it that—of knowing that he's a Peeping Tom.

"You raped that boy," I say aloud.

"Look," says the officer. "He does know you."

My blood boils when I hear this. "You fucker!" I say. "You did it again?" I pause, watch the man get behind the woman. "You did it again, didn't you? Didn't you?"

The woman pulls the pervert out of the room and closes the door tightly behind her. I'm left alone, except with Casper the friendly ghost here. "I can't believe, all of that shit and he got off again!"

"His charges were dismissed because of you."

"What?" I say back to Joey, who stands behind me, taunting me with his freedom. He walks around me, takes a step forward, then backward, knowing that I can't do the same.

"When the boy was shot, the man was acquitted. Illegal search and seizure, and all that jazz."

"That's bullshit!" I say. "Bullshit, and you know it."

"Do I?" says Joey. He sits on the floor and crosses his legs Indian-style. "Do tell."

"We weren't knocking in there illegally," I say. "We were," and then I pause and remember the moment of having Brandon not knock on the front door, the way he pulled his gun as he walked into the hallway and, without anything that even remotely resembled a clue, we walked into the room and tried to arrest the man because I fucked up the first time. Now I'm fucking up again. And again. And again.

"So you see, Robbie," he says, "if at first you don't succeed, then skydiving isn't for you." He points to me, flicks me on the nose. "In your case, policing isn't for you."

"You scrawny little shit, just you wait until I'm free, I'll fucking--" I say, but Joey cuts me off.

"Do what? I'm already dead. The worst thing you can do is," and he pauses, points at me, and he looks down at me, maybe embarrassed? It's too hard to tell through his hood. "Ahh, you almost got me there, Robbie." He points at me, chuckles to himself and then stands up. "You almost got me."

"Are you just sent here to torture me?" I scream.

Wilkes walks into the room as I shout this out at Joey. "No," he says. "I can't quite say that I am." He takes steady, confident steps to the table and sits opposite me. "But I'll keep that open as an option, if you'd like."

"Go to Hell," I say.

"We both know the outlook is that much greater if you'd just help us out, be honest," he says in his southern drawl. "And for Heaven's sakes, be kind and clean up the potty language."

I bite my lip, easy at first, but as all the things I want to call him pop into my head like whack-a-moles, I bite harder until I swear I'm tasting blood.

"That's a bit more like it," he says. "So you ready to speak now or should I come back in a little bit longer, give you time to reconsider the benefits of being forthcoming?" Wilkes rests his elbow on top of the desks and stares me into the eyes. I know he'll do it, he'll leave me. And Joey won't bother trying to spring me out, so I know I'll have to comply with his wishes.

"What exactly, are you going to tell us?"

"Nothing without a lawyer, you ass," I say. "Go fuck yourself."

"You'd like that, wouldn't you?" He gets up, his face goes white, then angry-red. "And I'm sure you'd love to watch," he says.

To keep from saying anything, I bite harder, but that barely does anything to keep me quiet, so I snort through my nose, make some kind of noise, some kind of release. I think I'm going to chew a hole right through my lip if I don't get out of here soon.

"And as I'm doing this, would that turn you on?" he says. "Would that turn you on, watching?" he says. "The Devil guides your hands," he says to me, whispering closely to my face. His gaze stays fixed on the door as he says to me, "You see, they should have never let you on the force, Officer Faggot."

"You don't know the first thing about me," I say.

"I know you and Brandon were partners, in more ways than one." He smiles as he watches my reaction, then pouts like he's upset that he called me out. "I'm sorry," he say, "but it's true. You're an abomination and a murderer, and I can prove it," he says.

"Where's my lawyer?" I ask. My ribcage can't seem to contain everything going on with me, so I pull my tears back. Keep them in my face and don't give him a chance to see me react. He can't win.

"He's on his way," he says. Wilkes takes a step back, pulls his sleeve back to check his watch. He says, "Maybe in about an hour."

"Then maybe I should wait," I say. "Unless you're charging me with something."

"Fuck it," he says. "I was trying to be nice, Lambert. Maybe let you confess and let you be the bad guy here, so I don't have to. But if you want to play hardball, then let's go ahead and do it." Wilkes walks to the door and opens it. "Can I get an officer in here?" He closes the door and then says, "I know we IA guys get a bad rap, but we're cops, too. Out of respect for the uniform, for our brothers-in-arms, I was going to try to help." He takes a swallow, then looks up, wondering how he's going to say this next part. "But you, you're just a rude, arrogant fag who doesn't think he can be touched." He takes a step back, puts his hands in his pants pockets to seem cool and in control. "But we can. We can get you."

An on-duty officer enters in the room. Wilkes points at me and says, "Detective Robert Lambert, you're under arrest for the death of Detective Brandon Jones." Wilkes points to the front door. "Take him to holding."

"And there it is," says Joey, invisible to even me, but echoing in my head.

FOURTEEN

I don't get to see a lawyer until my day of arraignment, where I'm charged with the murder of my boyfriend and partner, Brandon Jones.

"I'll see you in a few days," says Dean Schaeffer, the lawyer assigned to me. His accent isn't from the low country of South Carolina, it's from somewhere back in the Pacific Northwest. Maybe somewhere up north in Washington. A slight Canadian accent mixed that makes it sound like he doesn't have an accent at all.

"For what?" I ask.

"Good point," he says. He cups the cigarette in his mouth, lights it and takes a long drag. "You're fucked either way we do this, Robert. You do know that."

"You act like I'm guilty," I say. "Some lawyer."

"You're lucky I got them to drop bail," he says, takes another drag and then flicks the cigarette somewhere off into the emerald green grass just outside the courthouse. "You're not a potential flight risk, are you?"

"They don't seem to think so," I say, smile and wink at him.

He pauses, measures my body language and then squints as he says to my eyes, "I really hope you aren't." His hands go digging into pockets to find keys. "That was a lot of money, and that bail bondsman used to hunt crocs in the Louisiana bayou. I wouldn't fuck with him." He waves to me and steps across the street to a dark blue Honda Civic, probably early 2000s, and drives off.

My only car before the arrest was the undercover vehicle I borrowed from the department. Seeing as how I'm not in the department anymore, they confiscated the car for "evidence." That's code for "We're going to fuck with you until you cry." I'm all too familiar with those expressions. I used to do it myself. Once took a person's pet into custody, claimed it had blood on it from a murder that was supposedly committed. The man killed his wife, so we took his cat. Pissed him off, but it was funny as hell back at the office.

It's been about a full week, maybe eight days, since I've seen or heard from Joey's voice.

Part of me hopes that he's done messing with me.

Part of me misses that little bastard.

When I used to be a cop, only a few days ago, I could go about town, get something to eat and sometimes get free food or free dirty looks. The one thing I notice when I walk downtown to Little Teapot Café, is now I only get the dirty looks.

The waitress seats me up front and next to the bathrooms to the back and right of the front door. From where I sit, everyone has to walk right past me if they want to shit, piss, or wash their hands.

With each passing person, they stare or grimace or just cut the crap and give me the evil eye. If I believed in those types of things, I'd be dead ten times over.

The coffee comes out to me warm, not hot, with just a glimmer of something floating in the top of it. There's no love for suspected gay cop killers, especially if you're gay yourself. A small saucer of nondairy creamers comes to the table, and I pick out the pink packets, flick them against the back of my hand, and empty the contents into the coffee cup. The little granules swirl clockwise and then drop to the bottom of the coffee cup, too cold to dissolve, to warm to just float on top.

"Gee, thanks," I say.

The waitress comes back with a pen in hand, "Are you ready to order any food, hun?"

The word hun makes me stop stirring and I stare up at her. "No comments for me, today?"

"I'm sorry for the whole cold coffee and all. We ran out of the new stuff in the first carafe, so I had to give you this one. We can get y'all a new cup if you're wantin' one."

"So this was an accident?" I say. A sigh of relief escapes my chest, followed by a little chuckle.

"Well, not entirely an accident," she says.

"You know what I mean," I say and sip the luke-warm-and-getting-cooler-by-the-minute coffee and I actually like it. Brings out the sweetness. "Actually, this will be just splendid. But bring that new coffee here if you get some hot enough. This one might be gone a little too quick."

She miles at me, introduces herself as Donna, and then flicks her pen into ready position in her hand, locked and loaded for my order.

"Oh, I won't have anything. Sorry. I'm just looking for a place to get away for a while."

"Oh my gawd," she says and covers her mouth with her ticket book. "You're that guy, from the news?"

She puts the book down and shrugs, embarrassed by her behavior. "I'm sorry, but I thought I recognized you. You're cuter in person," she says. Her cheeks turn full red blush as she says under her breath—or so she thought—"It's true, all the cute ones are taken or gay."

"I'm sorry, excuse me?" I say.

"It's alright, honey. I know, and I'm okay with it. My brother is gay. Maybe I could hook him up with you sometime. I'm sure you're his type, too."

"No, really, it's fine. I'm just coming out of a relationship," I say.

"Of course you are," she says. "Want me to just find some pie I can scrounge up for you?"

The image in my head has her looking through other people's dishes and pushing a few pieces of half-eaten pie together to make one larger, regularized one. Colors of brown and green and yellow mish-mashed into some flavor combination that makes me want to throw up in my mouth a little.

"No, it's okay. Really."

"If you say so," she says. "And if you need, no hurry to get up on out of here. I'll check back with you as soon as that coffee is nice and warm." She disappears back behind the kitchen door and I'm left here with my thoughts, staring into the coffee and out into the window by my side. Nothing walks the side streets anymore, not since the news reports about cop killers and gays walking amongst them.

Never mind that Brandon's death was weeks ago.

Never mind that more convicted rapists and murderers are actually straight than gay. These backwoods hicks couldn't give a flying fuck.

My house gets attacked on a daily basis with eggs and toilet paper. Sometimes they'll spray paint something enjoyable and witty, like "God hates fags" on the wall. Sometimes they'll even spell hates and fags correctly. Leave it to modern teenagers to know how to spell masturbate correctly each and every time, and misspell fags. Go figure.

My thoughts return to the night of murder and my stay in the hospital room and my panic attack. Joey brought me there for a reason, I just don't know why.

I can't sit here and wait for something to happen. Goes against my nature.

Why, I was a pretty decent detective in this town.

Letting things go, Brandon used to say, was never one of my personality strengths. So it's no surprise to myself when I make the decision to pursue my ghostly friend. I believe I even know the first place to find him.

The second round of coffee takes too long to come back around, so I toss a five on the table and consider it a decent tip for being so polite to a suspected murderer.

When I leave the building, I shove my hands into my pockets. I catch the rest of my body language following this, huddling together not like I'm cold, like I'm trying to conceal myself. It's almost the middle of daylight when I leave the café, and it's going to be pretty hard to hide myself in a big ass street with no shade or trees on the sidewalks. Still, this amuses me, and I turn right toward the bridge that crosses the Columbus River.

People literally cross the street as they notice me coming.

We're not talking instantaneous recognition here. But once they get a glimpse of my profile, their expressions turn from curiosity to pure fear.

This is something you have to get used to. Those feelings of being watched, hated for who you are? Comes with the territory of being a cop. But when you start to think that you're going to get hurt, it's a whole other story.

Turns out they are more afraid of me than I am of them.

Now I cross streets when I notice they do. If they go to the next sidewalk over, so do I. Makes for some fun games of silent cat and mouse when I get bored. An older lady approaches me, her white hair in curls around her head as she walks her husband up the street. I don't know where they're coming from, but they are empty-handed and not going at a pace that says they need to get anywhere fast. The husband, I presume, walks slowly, hunched over slightly. His baby steps take nearly fifteen seconds to get in front of one another.

Perfect. I take extra care to lift my head up, look forward in their direction and smile. If there's anything I can count on, it's old people knowing what was on the news. The woman doesn't disappoint. She notices me and whispers something to her husband. I imagine the conversation goes something like, "There's that weirdo, Harold. Let's go over there." She stops moving and tugs on her husband's arm. With her body turning slightly at the feet, she drags her slow-moving man with her. They look as if they're about to cross the street, so I move first.

I look both ways like I taught hundreds of elementary kids to do over the years and then cross the street.

The woman, she looks dumbfounded as I beat her to the punch. Then, she does exactly what I expect, so I stop where I'm going and watch her go. I watch her go straight on until she comes to a stop and looks at me.

I wave back at her, wish her a good morning. The look on her face is priceless, something mixed with amazement and horror.

Then, I cross the street again, this time moving

directly toward them.

The woman, she doesn't know what to do. She stops and watches me come to her. Her loose rubbery lips drop open. Her feet face different directions, almost looking like she's dancing with her husband. She doesn't know what way to go, left or right. Straight ahead up the hill or back down where they came. It's a game of pedestrian chicken, a game I'm winning.

"You asshole," she says to me and huddles closer to her husband. If the husband is aware of this entire game, I can't tell, but he moves on up the hill toward the center of town, same as he always did before he saw me coming. His head faces the street, putting one foot in front of the other.

I stop in the middle of the street and watch the old man get himself where he wanted to go, and the wife, angry and watching me, protecting herself and her husband. She keeps a close, evil eye on me while I watch them in return.

The message is not lost on me.

Out of respect for the old man, his wife, and what they are trying to do, I lower my head and watch the few feet of asphalt in front of me and walk to the western side of the street, just behind the old lady. When she sees that I'm safe behind her, she keeps going, and I turn and go my opposite direction.

What did I become? What was I doing? Why did I think all of this was okay?

The old man didn't care what he was doing when I decided to freak them out a little. Either that or he was too out of it to tell.

Still, I guess I could learn a little something about all of this.

No more letting this affect me. I need to put my head down, figure this whole thing out. Fuck the police, fuck the games. Fuck this town.

And it's decided: When I'm done with all of this, I'm moving away. Far, far away from Saraday.

At about twenty-five feet from the front of the ice cream store, I stop and hear whimpers. Instincts command that I grab for my non-existent gun, but I stopped, listened, and froze where I stood.

"You can come out now, Robbie," says the whimpering voice. Joey takes a step out and appears in front of the store. "I already know you're there."

Of course you do.

"Where were you?" I ask. Small steps to the front door, then watching as Joey walks into the door, then disappears behind it.

"Here," he says, just barely loud enough for me to understand the syllables. "Always here."

"Is this your go-to place? Your happy place?"

"My blood lies all over the back office and soaked the desk. Who in their right mind would call this a happy place?"

Touchy. "Okay, then, Mr. Ghost. Sorry about that."

"What are you doing?" he says. His face turns to the back office. The hair on my wrists and neck begin to stand on end from the gradual chill that takes over the room.

"I'm looking for you," I say. "I need answers. I need to know what happened."

Joey's head turns away from me, so I walk to the other side of him. He turns his head again to keep me from seeing his face. "What's the point?" he asks.

"Great. A depressed ghost."

"We can't be depressed," he says, wipes his face with the back of his sleeved hand.

"Could have fooled me." I walk along the walls of the store, tracing the construction tools and pieces of shelving and wood lying around. "What's this place going to be?" I ask.

"Another ice cream store," he says.

"Your family is reopening it?" I ask with some hope in my voice. "That sounds great."

"My family moved away. They're not coming back."

I put the pieces together and nod. "Gotcha."

"So why here?" I ask. "Why don't you just move on to," I say. "Wait a sec. You can't, can you?"

"You're not as stupid as you look," he says. "Took you long enough."

"Why not?" I ask. "What's keeping you here?"

"You," he says. "You are the one that's keeping me here."

I shake my head, "I don't follow."

"You wouldn't," he says. His chest heaves up, then lets out a long sigh. "If I'm to move on, I'm to help you," he says.

"Great," I say. "Let me be helped." I stick my arms out into a Jesus Christ pose. "Let's go."

"You're an idiot," he says. His turns to look at me and his face, it's pale white. Paler, dirtier than before.

His skin looks thin as Chinese dumpling wrappers, pulled tight over his skull. The subtle nooks and mounds on his face look faded, almost pressed out by the tightness of his skin.

"What the hell happened to you?"

"Time is nearing," he says.

"I can't really tell you what's coming," he says. "But it's coming soon." He turns to me, takes a quick few steps. "Are you sure you want my help?"

"Do I have much of a choice?" I ask, and Joey

remains silent. His eyes, sunken and cold, have lost the life and playful exuberance that he used to have. No longer did he have the face of a seventeen-year-old boy. Now, with his black jacket and hood, he looked like death warmed over.

"Then come," he says, and extends a cold, pale blue index finger out of his sleeve and curls his finger toward himself.

At the sight of all of this, my skin crawls and I say nothing as I follow him to the back of the store and watch him lead me be. Once again, he does the floating thing, his legs barely moving while he seemingly hovers over the tools and pieces of wood.

"Where?" I ask.

Joey places a dead blue finger to his lips to tell me to shut the hell up.

I follow orders, though my common sense demands that I should run, run as fast as I can. That curious part of me, the one that Brandon cursed a million times, well it tells me that I need to see this through.

Joey pulls himself through the back door, then opens it from the outside. He says nothing, and his face shows no emotion, nothing but cold, frozen emotions.

This side of Joey I've never seen before, he pulls me forward with my hand, and then pushes me up against a wall. His body rushes toward me.

I flinch, pulling my eyes tightly shut and try to guard my face with my hands.

Whatever he's going to do, this is probably going to hurt.

His cold breathe envelopes my face—smells like nothing in particular, just cold air—as he says, "Open."

When I open my eyes, the rest of my body registers that we aren't in the back alleyway anymore. Joey's eyes—once sky blue, now a pale ice blue color—stares into me, through me, past me and he smiles. His teeth I can't see, but his cheeks pull upwards in my peripheral vision. All I see before me is his eyes. Those eyes, poisonous, beautiful eyes.

"Wakey, wakey," he says and pulls away from my body.

I blink, try to get my focus back as light cuts into my eyes, peels back my eyelids. Everything blurs for a moment, and then it doesn't. Everything is crystal clear, and we're outside of a cemetery. The local cemetery about five miles outside of the town's limits. This means in a blink of an eye, Joey traveled us nearly eight miles. Stone walls encircle the area, rounded at the tops and decorated with giant cement balls at every peak of the wall. The sign between the metal gate says "Saraday Catholic Cemetery" and the black gates lie open, waiting for mourners and visitors alike.

"Why here?" I say. A few steps back takes me to the very edge of the sidewalk where I nearly fall off into the street.

Joey's hand extends out to me, but then he freezes. "Not yet," he says. "Not your time."

And if Joey's sudden facelift gone horribly wrong didn't terrify me, that statement coming out of his mouth certainly did. I don't have words for this moment, but I allow myself to step forward and regain my balance on the sidewalk "Why here?" I ask again.

Joey ignores my request, pulls his hood up to his head and walks through the front gates, directly down the center of the black asphalt-paved road, and he doesn't look back to check that I'm following him.

"Why?" I ask again, this time louder. I'm following Joey, to where, I'm not sure. He shows no signs of even hearing me, so I shout louder over the traffic behind us. "Why?"

No response.

"Where are you taking me?"

He says nothing, but keeps walking forward with a mission. I follow and take in the piney scent of the trees from just outside the brick wall. The way everything smells wet and fresh. The silence of the hallowed grounds. All of this hits me the minute I get within two feet of the front gates, and it's all I can do to keep from losing track of Joey and just taking it all in.

The names along the side of the walkway don't mean much to me. Names I haven't heard of before. Family names like Flagg, Howe, Wolf. The headstones declare their owners as faithful husbands, beautiful wives, talented sons. Some are soldiers from World War II, others from the first World War. The thought crosses my mind about what my headstone would look like. What it would say, and just who would be willing to put anything together for me?

Joey takes a hard left as he walks down the road. I follow him, but stop to look at the flowers at the gravesite. Fake, since I can see the wires sticking out of the ends of the stem. They looked so real.

Back behind here are newer grave sites, recently opened in just the past few years since everyone was just dying to get in. The headstones don't look as sundried and faded. The letters are still visible, and nearly all are still shiny as the first day, I imagine.

I know he's not taking me to Brandon's site because Brandon wasn't buried anywhere here. After they found out about his death, his parents paid for his body to be shipped somewhere up north. Michigan, I want to say. Never met the pair, but from what I heard from Brandon, I wouldn't want to. Or so he thinks. I would have liked to have the honor of at least meeting them before they hated me. But Brandon feared they would refer to me as "that man who turned their poor baby queer."

Joey's pace picks up, so I run to catch up to his side and he takes another quick left, then a right. We're walking on small stones now, an artificial walkway designed to keep us off the grass and other people's faces. Joey's feet still don't appear to touch the ground. And it's this fact that keeps me focused on my own feet, taking quick and deliberate steps to be by Joey's side.

I'd ask where we're going, but he's already shown me that he won't answer.

Finally, Joey stops and turns to a headstone. He looks at me in my haste and takes a step backward. He's silent. Not even his shoes make a sound against the wet, just sprinkled grass. No signs of anything green even touching him. No chlorophyll on his shoes. No signs of wetness along his pant legs.

"What are we doing?" And as soon as the words leave my mouth, my eyes glance at the head stone. It reads Joey Fromberg. I stop breathing, catching my breath in my chest and bear-hugging it tightly against my ribcage. "You?" I ask.

Joey's head turns down, sad. Still, he says nothing.

I kneel down, take a look at his birth date and date

of death. "You're only sixteen?" I ask.

He nods. "Was only sixteen." That was over two years ago. "Today," he says. He's right. The day of death etched into the head stone read's today's date.

"I'm sorry," I say.

"You had nothing to do with this death," he says.

"What the hell is that supposed to mean?" I ask.

"We both know what," he says, and he turns and leads. "You said you were ready to come to grips with things," he says. His feet do that creepy floating thing. "You saw where I am, where my body lies. Now it's time to see where yours will lie."

FIFTEEN

Joey's feet don't move, but it looks like he's hauling ass through the cemetery and I nearly lose him as he disappears through a wall into a separate and less expensive-looking part of the grounds. The grass is still under the sprinkling system when I arrive around the wall. Joey is nearly thirty feet in front of me, and accelerating once he sees me pass by the wall.

If it's a race he wants, it's a race he'll get. I pick up my pace and sprint through the sprinklers. I run as much as these pants will let me. Water rains into my eyes, some of the sprinklers manage to hit me head on. A painful stream of water drags alongside my head like a dull ice pick.

My feet slip over the stone path, and they nearly slide off when I come to a complete stop. There is no traction underneath my feet anymore. All attempts to stop on my own volition have me sliding down the path on my butt, finally falling off of the stones and into the grass. I use my shoulders and elbows to get myself standing again and there's Joey, standing above me. "Are you done playing yet?" he says.

His hands materialize long enough to help me up, then he turns nearly translucent enough for me to look right through him. What appears is a blank spot in the corner of the walls.

"That's for me?" I say.

Joey answers my question by side-stepping and allowing me to get a closer look at the site. My hip hurts when I walk on my left side, the joint where my leg meets my butt bruised somewhere deep in the muscle. Maybe this is how I die, I think. Maybe I die here, this instant.

I turn around to make sure that crazy ghost doesn't try to give me a heart attack, maybe hit me with an axe or a machete and make me fall down to my own personal grave spot.

Instead, he stands still only ten feet away from me, watching my reaction.

"If this is where I get buried, why is it so still?"

"No one knows you're going to die yet," he says. That's comforting. Means I don't end up dying on purpose, I imagine.

"Not yet, anyway," he says. "You have twenty-four hours to do what you need to do."

"And then, what, you get your wings?" I say with a smirk.

Joey doesn't get the joke, instead turns his head and says, "No, I get my cloak."

"Cloak?" I say. The image of him in a cloak standing cold over someone else's body suddenly makes sense. "You're death."

"An incarnation, yes." He takes a few steps toward me. "When I died, this was where I found myself. I needed someone to help pass over to the other side before I could move on to my new position."

"Doesn't this break a bunch of rules?" I say. "I mean, it's not like anyone talks about meeting an angel, or an incarnation of death all the time."

"How many people do you know are meant to stay alive if they meet an incarnation of death?" he says. Joey grabs my shirt and drags me with him as he turns around and walks—this time I checked his feet—toward the front of the cemetery again.

"I showed you the probable ending of your

journey," he says. "Now it's time I show you how to get there."

Joey leads me to a bus stop where we wait for fifteen minutes for the next bus to come. Technically, this is beyond city limits, and I'm pretty damned sure that I am breaking the terms of my bond. Still, I don't hesitate to get into the bus and see just where Joey tells me to get off.

I find a seat sitting next to a middle-aged oriental woman. Japanese or Korean, I can't tell. But she hums to herself some tune I don't recognize, probably made up. She looks at me, smiles and then politely turns her head to the other direction, staring out the windows to emerald views of trees and swamp on the driver's side.

And this lady, she seems happy, smiling and content with life. If wonder, has she seen death? Has she ever experienced it? As a cop, I get to see it more often than most.

That's not bragging.

Nobody is ever made softer because of it. No one is ever made immune to the effects of death.

You either let it kill you inside, or you turn into a miserable mess, incapable of being a functional human being.

I fell into the second category. Most of the guys in the police force? They turned into the first kind:

Pretending everything is okay so they can go about their daily lives. We've shot and killed, taken lives. It's no different for us just because it's part of the small print on the job description.

This lady, one of the thousands I've sworn to protect and to serve, she gets up from the seat and presses the black strip along the bus's wall. She smiles again at me, nods and then walks to the front of the bus, going hand-over-hand on the railings until she gets just to the yellow line. The bus stops with a jerk forward, and the lady gets off. The street name is, I don't what. This lady steps off of the bus and walks down the street, opposite direction and still has the same smile on her face.

The seat next to me seems empty, and I realize that Joey isn't on this bus. If he is, he's not telling anyone.

The next few stops come and go, more people get on the bus, some people get off. I'm left wondering exactly where I'm going when I hear the stop sign chime inside, an electronic chime that tells the bus driver the next stop.

"This is you," whispers a voice into my ear. I follow directions, wave to the bus driver and step off, the same way the oriental lady did. She looked both ways the way you're supposed to, then walked along the sidewalk and minded her own business. She's alive and well.

Me? I'm going to die in a day.

Oh my god. I'm going to die in twenty-four hours.

"Joey," I say, mostly under my breath, but I won't apologize if anyone else thinks I'm talking to myself. I take a few steps forward, away from the bus stop to the south and wait for a response.

"Over here," says the voice. A tug on my shirt sleeve tells me that I'm moving in the wrong direction. Turning around, I take a few steps and cross the street. The traffic doesn't bother to stop for me, but the thought crosses my mind. What if they didn't? What if I did get hit? Is this when Joey was supposed to kill me? Is this when I die?

So, I do what any other sane person in my position would do: I asked him. I stop right there in the middle of the road, and I look to the sky, mouth open wide, and say, "Joey!" Traffic stops in front of me, cars honk like I'm some kind of crazy person. "Joey! Is this how I die?" I cup my hands around my mouth to give my voice more power and distance. "Is it?"

"Hey asshole!" shouts one of the drivers. "Get the fuck out the street! You trying to get yourself killed?"

And I think, the nerve of this guy. So I yell out to him, "Do you mind, sir? I'm trying to have an enlightening experience here!"

The man shouts back, "Can you have it on the side of the road, jackass?"

The man's question processes in my mind as a good one, so I cross the street and make one last call into the atmosphere. "Is this how I'm supposed to die?" I shout out.

"You're an idiot," he says. "And even if I wanted to, I can't tell you when you die."

"Then what good are you?" I ask.

Joey's shoulders drop. "Move," he says. His bony fingers point up the street past some business buildings and into a tree-lined street that turns residential. I hoof it since there is no other alternative. With no one to talk to, images of my would-be grave appear in my head. The feeling of the silk interior of the coffin touches my skin, and I'm at the same time comfortable and horrified of the darkness. My body lies still, waiting for who knows what. My arms are stretched across my chest, restful with a purpose.

He's full of shit. That image? It's way too ridiculous. "You're full of shit, Joey." His body doesn't bother to flinch or turn around as I taunt him. "You're full of shit. That back there? It wasn't my grave. It was just a blank plot. I'm on to you." If I weren't here, in the middle of nowhere, I swear I'd just turn around. Only to return later and wonder just what he was leading me to anyway.

I can't prove it, but I swear I see Joey pick up his pace. Not enough to lose me, but to piss me off.

"Real grown up, there, Joey. Real grown up."

I jog to catch up with my spirit guide and decide to tail him. Might be safer this way. I can always decide that shit's going to get too serious and just duck out. Maybe.

I follow Joey left into a subdivision, one of those subdivisions that were planned out by some association. The streets have synchronized names. These here are all based on Italy. Sicilian Drive. Pisa Plaza. Leonardo da Vinci Way. Cute. Very cute.

Joey's beeline takes us to the front of a small, one-story house with a small garden just under the living room window. The garden looks fresh, buds of some green just popping out of the soil.

"You keep bringing me to houses?" I ask.

Joey rings the doorbell and sidesteps the doorway, pointing at the ground or me to be in the direct line of sight of whoever opens the door. "Where are we?" I ask.

"The Parker residence," says Joey.

The door opens, and a woman, hair pulled back, looking frazzled and dry, looks at me with a worried smile. "Can I help you?" she says.

"Mrs. Parker?" I ask. "Is that you?"

"May I ask what this is about?" she says. Most of her body remains hidden behind the door, using it as a barrier between me and her should I try to get inside.

My hands reach for my back pocket, and I realize I don't have a badge anymore. "Um, I'm from the Saraday Police Department, ma'am." I swallow my pride and take the hint that I think I know what Joey wants. "And I believe we should talk about your son."

The door shuts in our face after Mrs. Parker's face turns beet red.

I place my face so close to the door that my cheek barely touches the paint. "Please, Mrs. Parker. Please, just open the door. We need to talk. I believe I have some information that may help you."

The door lock flicks shut, then open, I assume. Then, there's a jiggle of the handle that tells me that Mrs. Parker hasn't quite left the front entryway yet. I've caught her attention.

The door cracks open, and her eye pokes through. "What can you tell me about my son?" she says. "What can you possibly tell me about my son?" The door quivers from her nervous grip.

"Ma'am," I say. I put my hand on the door and try to push it open with a nudge, but she holds it tightly against her body. "Ma'am," I say. "I was there when your son was shot." I swallow a bit of the spit in my mouth, along with a little pride. "I was one of the arresting officers."

The door opens up completely, and the woman decides to let me in. She waves me in and fixes the bun in her head. The door shuts and Joey invites himself in by just walking through the front door, unawares to my hostess.

"What do you want?" she says. "We've already found the guy. We've dragged his good name through the mud." She motions for me to follow her into the living room where she offers me a seat with an open palm pointing to the loveseat. "What else do you want to do?"

"I believe that we don't really have all of the pieces quite into place, you see." A dozen thoughts creep into my head and demand attention in my brain. The internal dialogue among them all, it gets too loud for my ears, so I search from side to side to maybe get a sneak of where Joey is sitting. Maybe he's in the room.

Guide me, o Spirit Guide. Tell me what I should do.

From window to wall, I don't see any sign of Joey, so I continue without him. "We at the police department have determined that there were some inaccuracies in that particular report."

"But you were there at the scene, weren't you, officer?" she says.

"Detective," I correct her, but it's not really the time to nitpick. My heart doesn't just skip a beat, it leaps. It has to be painfully obvious as I try to recover. "Well, yes, I was." Pause and re-track my train. "I believe that I my partner was inaccurate in some of his reports."

"Your partner died in my house," she says. She sits down and crosses her hands in her lap. Not quite a power position, but one that shows confidence, or at least that she's having fun trying to make me squirm.

I clench my fists and fold them in my lap to keep from doing something stupid with them. I can't clench my teeth or show my increasing frustration through my face or risk getting kicked out of here. "Let me put it like this, ma'am, after having a few tests done, we believe that there is more that you should know about."

"Get out," she says. "There's no point in rehashing old information. I know what I heard, I know what I saw, and what's done is done. There isn't any reason to go back for it."

"But ma'am," I say, standing up and trying to keep my hands cupped together. "I really must tell you something."

"Then stop beating around the bush and just tell me," she says. "Just say it already and be on your way." She checks the clock on the wall by the front door. "I have to get dinner started soon." From the looks around the room, I'd say she probably lives alone, especially since her husband left her and the son is dead, but I don't bring up the technicalities.

"I'm trying to say it, but you keep interrupting me, ma'am." Try as I might, I can't keep from wanting to rip her face off. "You haven't quite given me the chance to say what I needed to say."

"I gave you plenty of time, and you wasted it. Now please," she says, showing me the door. "Please leave."

I hold my breath and turn to leave when there's the sudden burst of Joey in my head. "Say it, Robbie."

"There's nothing to say," I say aloud, unawares that it was not just in my head.

"Then why did you come?" she says. "As a matter of fact, where's your badge?" she says. "Am I going to have to call the cops?"

"I am the cops," I say.

"Your badge?" she says. She places one sassy hand on her hip, and the other is extended out to me. "Well?"

"They took my badge a few weeks ago, but I can explain."

"I'm calling the cops," she says and makes a quick

beeline to a cell phone on the dining room table behind her. "I can't do this. Not now."

Her fingers fumble over the number pad, and for a second she stops and stares at the phone like she's forgotten what she's dialing. Then, pressing three numbers into her phone, she puts it into her ear.

"Don't!" says the voice in my head, so I respond by running to Mrs. Parker's side and knocking her hand away from her head. The phone goes flying out of her grip, flipping into the air and cracking on the linoleum floor.

"I'm sorry," I say.

And she punches me. Hard. In the chest.

The part of me that isn't caught by surprise struggles to keep breathing.

"Do you want money?" she cries out. Her face has exploded with tears and mournful sobs. "I don't have any money," she says "I don't have anything."

She hits me again, again in the chest, and I just explode. I don't know why, but I see instant red and shout out, "God dammit!" and grab my arm like it's going to soothe the pain. Then without a thought, I scream at her, "You stupid bitch! I'm going to die, and it's all because you're not going to let me apologize for killing your son."

The woman's legs drop from underneath her. The

sounds of her hands slapping the floor echoes into the dead silence that followed my confession.

"I was the one that killed your son," I say. "Not my partner."

Mrs. Parker sits up, her face dirty with blood rushing to color the surface of her cheeks from the fall. Her elbows bend slightly, barely able to keep herself up. I kneel down beside her and offer her my hand. She slaps it off to the side and lets herself sob like she's been holding it in for years.

"Your son was going to kill my partner, my boyfriend, when I had to stop him."

Her bloodshot eyes peer up at me, gradual and slow. She takes slowly tilts her whole head upward, seeing my face head-on.

"I needed to protect him, so I shot your son. Not to kill, but to keep him from harming anyone." I try to touch her hand. "I'm truly sorry." The words come out easier than I thought they would. It's when the thought of whether Joey approves of this or not appears in my head when I feel a hand on my shoulder. I look up and back around to see Joey, not smiling but pissed at me.

"You're lying to her to save your ass?" he says.

I shrug him off and return my gaze to the quickly deteriorating Mrs. Parker.

"Why now?" she says. "Why do you do this to me

now?"

"I needed to get some of this off of my chest," I say.

"Bullshit," says Joey, but I'm apparently the only one who seems to hear him. "Bullshit, bullshit, bullshit," he says in a sing-songy voice. "Now apologize for real," he says.

"I don't know what you're talking about," I say.

Mrs. Parker flinches, the shakes her head free of the confusion. "What I mean is it's been this long, why come and tell me who shot my son?" She pulls herself up, sitting on her knees. "Don't you understand? I don't care who killed him. All that matters is that he's gone." She blinks, her bloodshot eyes disappearing behind red, sore eyelids from rubbing and crying. Her body language falls upon itself, giving up and giving in to the torrential wave of emotions that overcome her senses. Her emotions, they're so strong, even I feel them taking over this far away from her.

"I'm not talking to you!" I shout at her. Then, looking over my shoulder, I say, "Stop!"

"You're crazy!" she says, pointing at me, like I didn't know who else she could be talking about.

"I'm not crazy," I say. But then, thinking about explaining that I'm talking to Death itself—or one of them—would make me sound crazy, so I don't bother explaining. "Just let me take a second."

"You're just going to lie to her again," he says.

"No, I'm not!" I say.

"Yes, you are," he commands and disappears from the buzzing in my ears.

The woman, she crawls to the middle of the kitchen where her cell phone landed, picks it up and starts dialing as quickly as her eyes can find the buttons. When it starts to ring, she puts the phone to her left ear and says, "I have a crazy person in my house."

I can't do this. I can't just stay here, following a madman's whim and confessing to things just because some stupid ghost kid tells me to.

So, I get up, dust myself off and walk—not run— to the front door and let myself out. I figure even if the police were going to respond to the call, it would still take about ten to fifteen minutes to get there. Plenty of time for me to skip out, hide somewhere and wait for the coast to clear.

"What was that back there?" says Joey. Still invisible, probably walking behind me, I don't know.

If I say anything now, I'll just start another fight.

"You're a shitty detective, you know that?" he says, this time his words crawl inside my ear, almost like they echo inside my skull. "You pride yourself on solving the puzzle, never stopping until the truth is found. Now that it's time you admit the truth, you can't. You're a pussy and a shitty detective."

Those words make my feet stop moving, and I turn around to face—well, nothing really—and say, "So you think name calling is going to get you anywhere? Really?" No response, so I continue with the first words that come to mind. "You may be Death, but you're still a fucking punk kid who has no idea what life is like. No. Fucking. Idea."

A force that feels like a clawed hand grabs my chest from the inside, under my ribcage, and twirls me around. My knees buckle from behind, kicked by invisible feet. On my knees, my face is forced to the floor by hands I can barely feel against the skin on the back of my head.

Joey's voice digs deeper into my brain. Nearly cavernous echoes shout, "You have a fear of death that makes you reckless, Robert." Joey's skeletal face materializes from the concrete of the sidewalk and stays nearly half an inch from my face. "I will make you come to respect Death," it says. "You will come to respect me. Know me. And fear me."

I feel something throw me upwards, from facing the sidewalk to now staring into the sky.

I'm up off my knees, nearly airborne and hitting the back of my head against the edge of the street. The rest of Joey pulls himself out of the concrete, slow and creepy.

He stands before me, his jacket longer now, dark, waving in non-existent wind. "You will obey me, or risk living your afterlife here, tortured by your crimes."

What happened to the Joey I used to know?

"This, I command," he says. I blink, and there is Joey's bony hand in front of my face. His fingertips chill my skin where he touches me. His hand pulls backward, pulling my skin, my face forward and it hurts like hell. My skin being pulled from my face, I feel dragged forward. Each sharp crag of the sidewalk cuts into my arms and feet. The uneven pieces of the sidewalk pull on my pants. I can't use my arms, they're too busy trying to stop the oncoming concrete from attacking the rest of me, pushed forward in front of me and scraping off skin with every bump and crack.

I'm not even sure if I'm in control of my face muscles. Every piece of loose skin on my forehead, my cheekbones, and my jawbone has Joey's magnetic grip against it. He pulls it forward, so my words sound muffled when I say, "Please!" I cry out, "Let me go. I can help. I can do what you want."

Joey's walking pace turns into a running pace, fast enough so that my arms can't protect me anymore. Instead, the force of the drag causes my arms to fall behind me, victim to the bumps and scrapes of the rough sidewalk concrete. I feel every cut. Every scratch. Everything feels like it's cutting deeper and deeper. My skin against a concrete grater.

"I can help," I say. Joey's palm keeps me from knowing where we're going, or if anyone else on the street can see me. Maybe someone can go get help. "I can change. We can still be friends," I say.

Joey laughs, a deep chuckle. "You had your chance," he says.

My skin burns with searing scrapes and cuts. Beyond bruising, the rough surface of the cement shreds my skin, flaying me while I just try to go limp and not struggle.

"Just let me be," I say. "I'll do what you ask." I close my eyes as best I can. Joey's frozen grip against my face restricts most of my facial movement. Blinking requires my skin stretching like it's been pinned back three inches on all sides. I don't know if I try to laugh or cry out will I tear my own face off?

Joey remains silent.

My muscles begin to go limp. I don't want to fight any of this anymore. I can't do this. My grave awaits. The hole that's not dug yet. The casket that's not there. That will be my final resting place. The image in my head feels more real like it's right before my eyes.

And for the first time in what I can remember, I cry not out of frustration, but of fear. I cry because I know somehow, someway, I deserve this.

Every muscle in the front of my body aches, burns, feels stretched beyond their ability. Every flex of a movement, every flinch just causes more burning sensations, flaying of my skin and weakness that causes the rest of my body to collapse. All that remains active, the only thing I can control right now, is my mind.

A dangerous place to be without a guide, without anything to distract you.

The one thing I've been trying to fight this whole time. Distract myself with Joey. Keep from thinking about him. From feeling him. From feeling his loss.

A wet slick against my weak and lifeless forearms snap me back into the reality that I'm not on the street anymore. Grass.

Grass? Where would he take me that has grass.

The skin on my face relaxes, feels loose against the skull. This pleasant and welcomed sensation distracts me from the fact that my head drops to the ground, my jaw somewhat softening the blow. Teeth chatter and slam against each other. My head hurts like hell from my jawbone through my ears, pressure building up in my temples and into my eyes. When I blink, I see another gravestone in front of me.

"Where are we?" I mumble, doubting that anyone can actually understand my words. Even my tongue hurts to use it right now.

I roll over as best I can, but my exhausted abs don't want to. Using my shoulders as leverage, I flip myself over and stare directly into the afternoon sun. I don't know how much time has passed, but at this time, it's painfully aware to my damaged skin that these are the sun's most potent hours.

I blink and try to cover my eyes, but my shoulders cry out in pain when I attempt to lift my hands. "Where are we?" I ask again.

Joey's image comes over me, stares into my face and his face, it shifts from a recognizable flesh tone to pale. Bone-white pale.

The darkness created from his sunken eyes has created two twinkling stars where his sky blue irises used to be. Despite his standing above me, the sun still beats through him, onto my face. He opens his mouth and light appears through him, into my face. "We're at your final resting place," he says.

SIXTEEN

Joey's giant frozen hand grips my shirt and pulls me to my feet. I'm barely able to stand of my own volition, but I do a pretty decent job of wobbling back and forth until I can rest my hand against a nearby tree.

I have to wince from the pain when I bring my arm up to shield my eyes from the glaring sun. Cutting into my wounds, my skin already raw and grated open, I get the feeling I'm being baked as I stand here.

"This isn't a grave," I say.

Joey's form doesn't say anything, playing the stoic son of a bitch that is seriously pissing me off. Instead, he waltzes into the front door—or should I say through the front door—and disappears behind it.

I have no other option but to knock on the door with my bloodied knuckles. In the shade of the front of the house blocking the sun, I get a chance to see the caked-on blood forming on my forearms and knuckles. My pants look like I got into a fight with a lawnmower and lost. My shirt has been Swiss-cheesed by the sidewalk, and I hurt all over like I fell out of an airplane without a chute. The door opens up after I'm about to knock again. The inside of the house is empty of people but set up in a familiar way.

"Robert, what are you doing?" says a voice down the hallway. When I look down, to my right, down the dark wood hallway that has haunted my dreams and waking nightmares, I see Brandon with his gun pulled, held with both hands and pointing downward at the carpet. "I think this is it," he says. He motions over to me with a nod toward the door.

"This. Isn't happening," I say. "There's no way." I reach out a hand to touch Brandon's face, but he pulls away.

"What's wrong with you," he whispers to me. "Do you want to get this guy or not?" he says. Brandon turns his head to face the door, then rests his ear against it, listening for evidence or a reason to burst in.

"Get this guy?" I ask. "No, we can't." I put my

hands on Brandon's arm and get him to lower his gun. "We can't do this. Not here. Not now." I'm struck by the realization that my arms don't hurt, and my pants aren't shredded when I look down.

Is this real?

"What are you looking at?" says Brandon in a low whisper, and getting less whispery. The skin on his face turns pinkish on his cheekbones, a sure sign that he's getting frustrated. His neck will turn red next if memory serves.

What I'm looking at, or trying to look at, is Joey, who is in the perfect position that I can't see him directly, but his body appear fuzzy and translucent through the corner of my eyes. "Nothing," I say. "I can't believe you're alive."

Brandon grabs my shirt and drags me to the front door again, away from the hallway. "Are you okay?" he says. "You're not on something? Take something in the car?"

"I'm fine," I say and lean over to kiss him on the lips. His lips don't move to meet mine, feel stiff and unwelcoming. "What's the matter?"

"What's the matter with you?" he says.

"I love you."

Brandon's eyes check me over from toe to head. "Are you okay?" he says.

"Joey, what are you doing?" I ask.

Brandon's face turns to horror, then shock. His eyebrows raise. "Who the hell is Joey?"

"No one," I say. "I didn't say Joey."

"No, you said Joey," he says. He presses me against the door and whispers to me. "We'll talk about this later."

Brandon's neck is full red-hot red, so my heart flutters, then pounds as he takes confident but cautious steps to the bedroom door again.

"Let's go," I say. Say, not whisper, so Brandon's look of "hush" doesn't come as much of a surprise to me. What does come as a surprise is the naked man who opens the door.

"Who the hell are you?" he says, or tries to say before Brandon shoves him to the ground with his elbow.

"Freeze!" Brandon says, then enters into the room, pointing his gun to the four corners of the room and then looking at me, nodding for me to come in.

None of this happened the first time we went in. I know this. My memory isn't wrong.

We're not reliving my memory, are we, Joey? Where the hell are you?

I sprint to the front door and pull my gun from my back waistband and point it at the kid, who's naked and spread out on the bedspread. This boy, he's Joey-but-not-Joey. This ghostly person following me yesterday, taking Joey's persona, this is him.

The boy grabs for a sheet to cover himself up. His wide opened eyes nearly match the size of his open mouth. This look of shock, I guess I'd have the same expression if two guys came into my bedroom guns blazing in the middle of sex.

"Don't move a muscle," says Brandon. He points his gun first at the man, then at the boy, then the man.

"What do you want?" says the man.

"It's okay, Trevor," I tell the boy on the bed. "We're not here to hurt you."

"You fucking know this kid?" Brandon says, surprise just dripping off his voice.

I ignore his question. "We're not going not going to hurt you. Do you have clothes that you can put on?" I ask.

He nods, then motions to the floor between the bed and the wall. Real tacky, but I nod and motion for him to get dressed. I then direct my attention to Brandon, who's still holding this man at gunpoint and getting closer and closer. The man's gone totally soft down there, and trying to cover it with his hands and hold himself up at the same time. It's a losing battle. It seems since it just looks like he's rocking himself back and forth.

"Brandon, let's just calm down," I say. I raise my hands up, show them that I'm putting my gun down, when I hear a click and a thud against the wall.

To my right, Trevor has his pants on, no shirt, and he's pointing a gun right at me and Brandon. Without our uniforms on, they think we're robbing them, maybe just casual gay bashers, or serial killers. The potential list could go on and on.

"We're not going to hurt you," I say. "Put the gun down, Trevor." I continue to bend downward to the floor, showing him that I mean no harm, but Brandon points his gun at the kid.

"Don't be stupid, boy," my boyfriend says. "Put it down, and you'll both walk out of here alive."

"What the hell did you just say?" I ask. This begins to play like a movie reel in my head. All of the action looks celluloid in my vision. I don't feel like I'm in control of anything anymore, my actions controlled by my higher power. Only instinct takes over, an instinct to keep the peace and prevent anyone from getting hurt. "Brandon, stand down," I say.

Brandon raises his gun up at the boy, then smiles as he aims the barrel of the gun at the head of the man. "Don't be stupid," he repeats.

"Brandon! This isn't funny!" I say. The man tries

to push himself back against the wall, maybe thinking that he can crawl out of the room. Mistakenly of course. With two men with guns and a crazy young lover, nothing seems possible anymore.

"Brandon," I say. "Don't do it." I'm only half bent down when I realize that I'm still holding the gun.

The rest of this plays out like a script, not real life. Someone must be pulling my strings because I'm acting and watching myself at the same time. Moving, pulling my gun on my boyfriend and threatening him.

Trevor, he pulls the gun over on me, then to Brandon. His gun wavers in the air. His nerves are taking over, and every cop knows that sign means he's dangerous.

"C'mon, Trevor. You don't have to do this," I say. "Just put it down."

Tensions run high, and sweat trickles off his forehead onto the bed. "Get the fuck out," he says. "Leave us alone."

"We're cops," says Brandon. "We don't go anywhere."

"Brandon!" I try to catch my boyfriend's attention with my eyes, but he refuses to look at me. Instead, he moves his gun to point at the boy. His finger inches to the trigger. The tip of his finger nearly curls around it. "Trevor," I say, "if he has to, he'll shoot you. But none of this has to happen."

These words, they aren't mine. Not mine now. They are the words of a Robert Lambert from over a month ago. A Robert who is now being watched, playing like a memory in slow motion.

"Drop it," says Brandon. "Final warning."

The boy's gun wavers even more, shaking and jiggling in his hands. Trevor's grip looks like it's about to loosen, maybe drop the gun completely, but Brandon doesn't take the chance. Tension's too high for everyone.

I look to Brandon and try to tell him to put the gun down that Trevor's going to drop his. Instead, I see Brandon turn his body. His right index finger pulls the trigger. A bullet fires with a bang into the rapist's head. Blood squirts forward, then drips slowly from the wound in the man's forehead.

"What the hell are you doing?" I say, but not soon enough to stop him. Brandon points his gun at Trevor, and my head snaps to watch a bullet pierce Trevor's shoulder and splatter blood on the wall behind him.

A second bullet leaves the chamber and rips into Trevor's chest while he's still standing. Trevor's body goes plastic mannequin still, then relaxes. His eyes roll upwards, and his body goes limp, drops to the bed and his knees hit the bedroom floor with a thump.

Rage. Seething rage and regret and tightness in my chest takes over. My heart pumps this seething hatred for my partner's actions and I turn my gun on him and pull the trigger.

Adrenaline or the rush of what transpired, I don't know what motivated me. In that instant that I saw Trevor slump to the floor, I saw the face of every child I had ever failed to protect. I saw the faces of missing children, murdered women, mothers, flashing like Missing Persons posters in my head. Their bloodied faces, the pale lifeless cheeks. All of this flickers before my eyes like someone flips through a deck of cards.

Every person I couldn't save. Every damaged personality that turns to sex and drugs and crime for security, for safety, for meaning. Every woman and child's safety and vulnerability exploited, trusts shattered. Self-esteems destroyed.

Boys who become rapists themselves to deal with the pain. Girls who slit their own wrists to control their lives. I've had dozens of these cases since the sickos moved in to Saraday. Nice and secluded and virtually underground from law enforcement. This became the most popular crime of choice for white redneck sons of bitches.

When I pulled the trigger, I heard the cries for help from Sally Evans. Her dressed pulled up, her waist and ass fully exposed, she clutches her chest for security, crying for someone to save her from the evil stepfather that later raped her mother. The first one I failed. The first one I knew we just couldn't protect.

I saw more faces.

I just couldn't take it. I had to protect the child. So I shot my partner.

A single bullet goes through Brandon's head, point blank. The would-be rapist becomes the lucky recipient of Brandon's gray matter and skull fragments over his face and naked body.

My arms shake from the nerves. My legs twitch, vibrate. My heartbeats pulse harder, rushing rapids through my blood system. I feel my jugular vein pump blood, my whole neck pump pump pump.

I watch myself lower my gun, tuck it between the back of my shirt and the waistline of my pants and I step toward the door.

I don't grab a body, I don't call anyone. No emergency medical assistance. I can't be traced here, it'd end my career, destroy me.

I watch me leave the bedroom, panic pushing my heart harder, forcing my legs to fumble through the walkway. My legs try not to buckle underneath me, and it takes all of the focus I can muster to get to the front door. One step at a time.

Outside, I close the door quietly and try to pretend that I haven't just killed someone. Look casual. About as casual as a drunk frat boy appears on the street.

I have to make quick bursts of motions if I want to accomplish anything. Trying to focus against my nervous twitches and panicking body only seems to slow me down.

So I watch myself make large sprinting steps to the car. I try my hand at the door, but it's locked. The keys still lie in the pants pocket of my bleeding and dying boyfriend.

Oh god. Dying. He's dying.

But one step at a time. Get home. Do something. Get cleaned.

That's what I'll do.

I sprint under the dark sky to the next closest street and walk home. I take backstreets, trace the sides of buildings to remember where I can possibly get home.

The pacing is slow, but I manage to increase the distance between the bodies left to die, and me, struggling to not have a panic attack, to not break down. Caught up in a need to take a breath, I stop next to a store and hold myself up against the window. I wipe the sweat from my face, but when I lower my face, I see that it's not sweat, but blood. Brandon's splattered blood.

I use my sleeve to clean off my face, and I actually consider taking off my shirt, but the cold air and my hardened nipples keep me from following through on that thought.

I take a few more paces, and my legs strengthen their commitment to get me to safety. No longer am I feeling wobbly and walking on noodles.

"They deserved it," I say. They all deserved it. They shouldn't have been fucking. He shouldn't have been fucking a boy. Brandon shouldn't have dragged me there. We should have left well enough alone. He got off the charges. He was not guilty. My bad. My fault.

It was all my fault. I was willing to live with it. That's why I lived.

They died because they got selfish.

These are the things I tell myself, over and over again as I walk back to my house and let myself in through the back door. Never locked—and then I realized that I probably should from now on—I squeeze in through and go directly to the shower.

Here, I take my clothes off, leaving a trail from the front door of the bathroom to my dresser drawers, back to the bed. My sweat-drenched underwear and socks scattered across my bed. The blood-stained shirt on the floor—to be destroyed later after I'm cleaned.

My pants, I'll check for splatter later. There has to be something.

I don't pay attention to the temperature settings of the showerhead. I just turn everything on, until the needle-like water beats the tension, the regret, and the worries out of me.

The water rolls down my back, down my ass crack and the sensation tickles. A different feeling, not numb or regret, so I focus on that. My eyes close and everything feels sensitive. The water rolls down—no, cascades—down my back and rolls off in a mini-waterfall to the basin of the master shower.

Hands, darkened hands, slap against the door, which shakes and jolts me out of my dazed attempt to center myself. The hands slap against the door again as if trying to keep their owners from falling down and sliding down the frosted shower glass.

This is different from before. Not the memory in slow motion. This is new. What's real?

I blink, turn my head and realize that I'm suddenly inside my own head again, no longer watching myself play out a scene. I'm in control now. In control, and this frightens the shit out of me.

When I look to see who the hand is, I back myself up against the opposite end. It won't offer more protection against an attacker, but the rest of my body isn't thinking right now. Only acting.

"Who are you?" I say, grabbing the shower head and pointing it at the front door. I pull it open and let the shower stream all along the bathroom floor. Puddles collect, water hits the cabinets and bathroom counters, but no one is there.

After turning the shower off, I take a cautious step out of the shower, then step out. I reach for my towel, always hanging on the left end of the towel rack, and wrap it around my waist. My body shivers from nerves and the cold bathroom air caressing my body.

"Who's there?" I ask. I have no weapons, so I make fists and hold them directly in front of me. No one makes a noise, so I hold my breath and listen in closer. No response. "Hello?" I ask once again. "Brandon?"

Of course, it's not Brandon.

Police, maybe? The department came by to tell me about his death?

"Just a minute," I say, loud to make sure that I'm being heard in all areas of the house. If someone is in here robbing me, I want them to know they are not alone. I reach for my gun on the bed and check to make sure the safety is off. "I'm coming, and I'm armed," I say.

I ease myself against the wall by the doorway. I listen, holding my breath, for any signs of thieves or cops. Nothing. Maybe they are listening for me? Frozen like I am?

I pull my gun tight to my body and point it out the doorway, then step out, looking down the hallway to my left, then to the right where the living room is. Nothing different. No intruders.

"You're pathetic," says someone behind me.

"Joey?" I turn and shoot. The bullet goes through Joey's body, passes right through without injuring him and makes a nice .44mm hole in my wall.

"Confess," he says.

Everything comes clear, and tears well up in my lower eyelids, then drip down my cheeks. "I'm sorry," I say.

"Confess," he says again. Joey's face becomes clear under the lighting, his skin faintly glowing a pale, dead white under his hood. "It's time," he says.

The towel nearly falls off of me when I drop to my knees. I sob, the crying coming so forcefully it folds my shoulders forward, big heaves as thick streams of tears well up and fall down my face.

I needed to stop having panic attacks about death, I told Joey. The reason why I became a cop, I meant. I needed to know what it was to be in control. Those words, everything, was truth.

"Time?" I ask when I look up to Joey and the

muscles on the left side of my chest seize. Tiny bursts, sparks of tingle, then numbness, travel down my left arm.

The signs aren't unknown to me, so I try as best I can to get to my cell phone in my pants pockets, back in the bedroom. But the pain, the pressure against my chest prevents me from focusing. Like having an elephant sit on your chest, the pressure makes me feel like my heart will explode any minute now. I have to hurry.

With my right arm, I drag myself to the bedroom. My gun was lost somewhere in the living room. My towel sticks to the floor thanks to friction and my bare ass is left trying to crawl to the bedroom.

When I make it to the doorway, I pull with my right arm, push with my legs. I can barely breathe. My lungs don't want to fill with air long enough for me to be comfortable. I wheeze heavy gasps for breathe as I try to stand up and make it to my phone.

What I see sitting on my bed when I get myself standing causes me to fall back down again. The pain is too great for me to ignore, so I clutch the left side of my chest.

Brandon sits up from the bed and hovers over me. "It's time," he says, then flashes a smile that doesn't give me peace or relaxation. It fills me with fear and terror and beads of sweat fall off my forehead.

What now feels like the pressure of two elephants sitting on me builds into my chest. "Please," I say. "Call for help."

Brandon doesn't budge, but that smile stays on his face. Taking no chances—hey, maybe this is just a hallucination—I turn to grab my pants, but they taunt me just beyond my reach.

"Please, Brandon. Help," I wheeze through the pain.

A sudden realization of death and dying and my end floods my brain. Where will I go? What will happen.

My hands flap around until I'm finally touching the denim of my pants. My fingers claw at the pants, pulling them toward me, feeling for pockets and scrape at something hard and plastic.

Maybe I'll survive.

Above me, Brandon is joined by Joey. "It's okay," he says.

"I'm sorry," I wheeze. "I'm sorry for—" but the rest of the sentence fails to leave my mouth. My brain still functions, processing the sounds of everything around me. The silence, then the knocking on the front door. I try to cling to the sounds of the knocking, thinking that maybe I'm making enough noise for someone to hear me, but I can feel something pulling at me, my soul, my consciousness, from the other side.

SEVENTEEN

A familiar beep drags me awake, but it hurts too much to open my eyes. So, I listen to the goings on around me. The plastic-against-metal sound of curtain rods moving and shoes tapping on tiled floors.

That Listerine smell of cleanliness.

Either I'm alive, or Heaven is a hospital bed.

I try to pull my eyes open, but everything around my forehead and in my face feels weak and lifeless. Listening for more signs, I catch a voice of a woman telling someone that I'm moving. This is news to me, so I pry my eyes open, forcing the muscles in my eyes to finally give in. The light blinds me at first, but eventually darkens and a woman stands over me, smiling.

"Welcome back, darlin," she says. Her cheeks are bright, blush-pink, and her face radiates happiness, which makes me worry more than be relieved to be alive. "You're okay," she says, sensing my confusion. "You had a panic attack and a mild cardiac dysrhythmia." She takes my hand, feels for my wrist and glances at her watch. "You're better now, though," she says. "Someone must be watching over you."

Yea, watching over me.

I nod and turn my head, looking around at my surroundings. No flowers anywhere, so no one seems to have missed me. I can live with that.

I have the room to myself, apparently. No one wants to share a room with a dead guy, I guess.

"Thirsty," I say. My chest muscles refuse to let me breathe too deeply. One word sentences for the time being.

"Of course, dear," she says. She sets my wrist gently on the bed and leaves the room for water.

Everything is oddly silent inside my room, not a feeling I'm used to. The view outside the open door reveals a busy desk and people in blue and maroon scrubs pacing back and forth, handing off charts or picking them up.

What catches my attention, however, isn't the

hustle and bustle outside, but the faint figure of a hooded person, only about five-foot-five standing at the end of the hallway. The shape of the hood denies me the benefit of seeing who he or she is, but the body language gives me clues.

"Thank you," I say faintly under my breath.

What I thought was my time wasn't actually my time. Maybe the boy took pity on me. To survive, I had to deal with Death himself.

How many people can say they lived to tell that tale?

Joey's figure turns around in the hallway, takes a few paces forward and disappears into the doors. His long grim reaper-esque cloak flourishes behind him as he twirls. Then finally it, too, disappears behind the doors.

The cloudy sky allows just a few rays of light to break through into my windows. My nurse comes back in and hands me the paper cone of water with a "Here you go, sweety."

I take it and sip the water, let the cold rush through my chest and cool my stomach linings.

"So how are you feeling, love?" asks the nurse. "Anything I can get you?"

"No," I say. "I'm good, thank you."

The woman promptly leaves my room after patting my arm, as if to say "Good job."

For the first time in months, my brain gives me permission to relax. In order to take advantage of the situation, I turn my head and close my eyes. Freedom is knowing that you won't wake up with nightmares, knowing that you aren't afraid. I close my eyes with that same knowledge, knowing that I'll be able to move on when I wake up.

ABOUT DAVID GEARING

DAVID GEARING writes and teaches in Southern Arizona, where he lives with his always supportive partner and loveable, needy cat.

As always, thank you for reading.

www.ingramcontent.com/pod-product-compliance
Lightning Source LLC
Chambersburg PA
CBHW070743180626
46818CB00007B/2964